AF872512

Love People

WARNING

This book contains loud noises and flashing images which may upset you. It also leads down unpleasant corridors in your brain. Please read responsibly.

Impressum

2. Auflage, 2023

Verlag Akademie-der-Abenteuer
Boris Pfeiffer, Pfalzburger Straße 10, 10719 Berlin
www.verlag-akademie-der-abenteuer.de
© 2022 by Verlag Akademie-der-Abenteuer
Alle Rechte vorbehalten.
Nachdruck, auch auszugsweise, nicht gestattet.
Cover: Verlag Akademie-der-Abenteuer unter Verwendung
Einer Illustrationen von Andy Siege
Satz von Maryam Andaz
Gedruckt und gebunden von BoD GmbH, Norderstedt
ISBN 978-3-98530-092-1
Printed in Germany

Bibliografische Information der Deutschen Nationalbibliothek:
Die Deutsche Nationalbibliothek verzeichnet diese Publikation in der
Deutschen Nationalbibliographie; detaillierte bibliografische Daten sind
Im Internet über http://dnb.d-nb.de abrufbar.

Love People

Andy Siege

VERLAG Akademie DER ABENTEUER

Inhaltsverzeichnis

CHAPTER ONE

Charlie is lying on the big black couch in her checkered boxer shorts and an old black T Shirt which has no motivational quote on it. She is on her phone, texting instructions to the office. Her instructions are always on point and allow her subordinates to get the job done.

Her hair is short and slick and combed to the side. Her boyish face is serene and her feminine lips neither pout nor smile.

She writes instructions to her subordinate regarding a budget proposal for a big project.

It had been raining and the petrichor blows in through the window and also a quality of light that flows like a rainbow.

Her subordinate answers: "It's too much money. They'll never give it to us."

There is a single sequoia tree in the yard outside. She wishes that she was closer to it. That she was living in the woods, away from the responsibility of technology. In some African forest with elephants and lions.

The TV is on and some star is rotating and emanating rays of light through the screen.

Charlie's girlfriend Tammy waddles in, dressed in pink. Mostly pink. With pink tights and a baby blue top. Her blonde hair in pigtails and with a pink superhero cape. Tammy is 18 but acts like a kid.

Charlie is 24 but acts like an older man. It kind of works.

The girls seem to even each other out.

Tammy says in a baby voice, "I want to go shopping."

Charlie asks what Tammy wants to buy.

"Clothes. I'm meeting Emily and Rodolfo at the mall and we want to buy something cute and have lattes."

Charlie tells Tammy that she won't give her too much money because she would spend it all.

Tammy snuggles up to Charlie. Charlie embraces her like a protector on the black couch.

"Please. I just want to go shopping."

Secretly Charlie's heart is dropping. She believes that Tammy should express herself freely and for that she needs to feel protected. But Charlie can't always just protect.

She gets another message: "We're not going to get this amount of money. The jury won't give it to us. There's too many like us. We're nothing special."

As Charlie is reading this bad news Tammy probes again. She says "All I need is a 100 dollars. I'll buy something cute. You'll like it. You'll see."

Charlie loses it for a moment, and fires up like a rocket. "Can't you see that I'm fucking busy." She pushes Tammy away and Tammy falls off the couch and hurts herself.

"Ouch" Tammy rubs her elbow and tears well up in her eyes and her face goes pink.

Charlie feels the hot anger coming off of Tammy. Tammy can get angry. Oh how she can get angry. It's like a heat wave. In that moment, Charlie feels like a jellyfish in the sun. Flabby and useless.

"Fine." Says Tammy. "You push me away? I leave."

Charlie says sorry and asks to talk about it and tries to explain the money situation but it's not what Tammy wants to hear.

Tammy says: "I don't want to hear it anymore. I've had enough."

Tammy storms out, her pink cape fluttering and Charlie sees her walk down the path past the sequoia into the distance, the window frame making it look like a gif on a cellphone screen. And the image loops in Charlie's memory.

And this time its final.

Charlie receives a message from her subordinate: "We have to start again from scratch. The last two years were a waste of time."

Charlie's hands shake and rub the sides of her beautiful boyish face and her feminine lips quiver and she runs her fingers through her short slick hair.

And she despairs at the loss of love and meaning.

CHAPTER TWO

Dmitry is 30 years old and lying supine on a comfy couch. It is 5pm and his boyfriend, Bob, is about to come back home from work.

Dmitry is wearing booty shorts but feels that his butt is too big. The rest of his body has become too round as well. He is clean shaven and has dyed blonde hair and a cherub face.

He wags his legs left and right and scrolls down instabook. He flicks past cute girls in butterfly outfits or with bunny ears. Their swimsuits barely hide the shape of their sex. These forms and colors fascinate him. He used to play with dolls when he was a child.

He used to be pretty like them. He feels that if he was more like that again then his boyfriend Bob would give him more love. Things have become difficult lately. Bob no longer makes Dmitry feel secure.

Outside in the sky the sun is an orange.

He hears Bob's heavy footsteps down the hallway, thudding towards their apartment rhythmically and Dmitry's heartbeat thuds along loud and gets louder the louder the footsteps get.

The clinking of keys and the door opens. Dmitry sits up and arches his back and lifts his chin to look like Grace Kelly. His heart is pounding. Pounding! He asks Bob how his day was.

"It was ok."

Bob is a filmmaker. He lugs around heavy cameras all day, is 40 years old and extremely hairy. They say that men only get stronger with age and with Bob this is the truth. Bob has broad shoulders and long, muscular arms and a wide back. Bob films scenery for a nature channel. He films butterflies and bunnies amongst the hills and the trees and below the orange sun.

But Bob hasn't noticed in a while that Dmitry is also as pretty as a butterfly. So Dmitry gets up gracefully and prances towards Bob and tries to give him a passionate kiss. But Bob pulls back his head.

"No. Not now."

Bob lugs his camera into the backroom. Dmitry's heart sinks.

When Bob comes back he ignores Dmitry again and enters the kitchen where he does some crack. Crack. Craack. Then he starts digging in the refrigerator.

Dmitry pouts his lips and hangs in the doorway seductively. His fat making him look feminine. He asks what the matter is.

Bob gives him no more than a dismissive glance. "Nothing. Where's all the food that I made yesterday?"

Dmitry drops his act and his face loses its playfulness. He tells Bob that he ate it.

"The whole lasagna? For fucks sake." Grunts Bob.

Dmitry tells him that he was hungry.

"I'm hungry too. And now I have to cook again."

Dmitry tells him that he will bake.

"No baking please. No more of this princess bullshit."

Dmitry is utterly shocked. His mouth drops open and he raises his hand to his breast.

Bob looks at him and hisses. "You're not 18 anymore. You don't look the part. You're getting fat. You're lazy. All of it."

Dmitry realizes that things haven't been alright for a while. He realizes that Bob has been speaking to him this way for a long time. All he wanted was a Damn Gina.

This isn't right. He picks up an expensive looking camera that's lying on the counter and throws it at Bob. Bob successfully ducks the projectile but the camera breaks against the fridge.

Bob's right, Dmitry isn't 18 anymore. His 30 year old man strength allows him to flip the couch. He becomes a whirlwind. He breaks things all over the living room. Crash there, crash there, craash!

Big muscular Bob lunges over the broken furniture and punches Dmitry in the face. Smack. Smaack! Dmitry's legs give out and he lands plump on his fat buttocks and he feels like a mermaid on land.

His eyes widen in fear and he is about to cry as he looks up at his assailant. His old man. His boyfriend. His partner.

Bob stares down at him spittle running from his mouth, his strong and wiry frame tense. Tense.

"Don't you dare call the police! I'll kill you if you do. Get out. Now!"

Because Dmitry has a hard time getting up he rolls over onto his side first and then uses his knees and arms to push himself up. His booty shorts, which were too tight to begin with rrip down the back.

Dmitry has barely got his footing when Bob shoves him towards the door. Dmitry asks about his things. His clothes, his electronics.

Bob says: "I'll throw them out to you."

And he does. Dmitry is sitting on the lawn outside below the orange sun, his things floating down around him. Lots of pink and baby blue and the occasional crash of a mobile device or a tablet or the clink of a ring or a pendant.

CHAPTER THREE

Charlie can't do solitude. She's had enough throughout her life. She needs to get off the couch, which is by now covered in chocolate wrappers. She watched a series marathon and tried reading a book, but it was too long.

Charlie puts on a blazer and does her hair. She pouts her lips and takes a video in the mirror. In the video she bares her teeth and moves her eyebrows. She then picks the best three seconds for her brushwood profile.

Even though all her deals have gone south and she won't have money for a while, she splurges a little and pays 6.99 for more visibility.

The chat requests pour in. She picks three girls that look like Tammy. Petite and blonde. She writes them for a while.

The first is a gold digger and asks "how much money do you make?"

The second seems unsure about her sexuality. "So do you consider yourself a boy?" she asks. As if she was doing this for the first time and Charlie doesn't want anything to do with that.

But the third girl's got her shook. The third girl writes "Ouch, my heart." When Charlie talks about Tammy.

Charlie agrees to see her. In her profile picture she's wearing a short green top and baby blue booty shorts and her blonde hair is in a ponytail. Her name is "You". Charlie can't wait to get to know her better. She likes to inspect the girls she dates, past the fire and the flesh down to the bone. To inspect their rolling hills and taste of their river. To calmly kill them with her tongue. And then to ignite their leaves again until they become a burning tree that speaks only truth.

Charlie fancies herself as a kind of pussy guru.

Charlie goes to meet with You.

She dresses up and takes an Under to the Triangular Bar. You arrives late, as is customary for girly girls.

Charlie sits at the bar and calmly drinks a glass of whiskey. She does her best to look composed and masculine and ready for a fight. It is early in the evening and there aren't a lot of other girls around.

You walks in the door and is beautiful. She immediately sees Charlie but then pretends to look around for a moment with a hidden smile. That's a good sign, thinks Charlie.

Charlie waves and You comes over.

"Hi I'm You".

Charlie introduces herself as well and then buys You a drink. Charlie really likes You's femininity. It makes her feel masculine. They converse for a while. Charlie talks for a moment about Tammy and their breakup. You listens and then turns it around and begins speaking about her own issues. She does this for Charlie. To make Charlie a guru again. Charlie notices this and likes it.

After the bar they go for a walk. There's large groups of people outside. Drunk. Shouting at each other. Shoving each other. Charlie feels her heart begin to pound. She definitely doesn't want to get into a fight. She doesn't want to get hurt and she doesn't want You to get hurt.

But in that moment You begins to sing like a nightingale and draws attention to the two of them.

"for ramblin for rovin for football and sportin‘
for drinkin‘ black porter as fast as you fill
in all you days rovin‘ you‘ll find none so jovial
as the Muskerry sportsman the Bold Thaddy Quill"

Charlie shushes You. Some men look over at them. They have dark hair and dark features and cruel mouths.

"Hey girls. What can we do for you?"

Charlie senses aggression in the tone and takes You's arm and tries to walk in the opposite direction with her. But You shakes herself free and continues singing, this time at the men and at the top of her voice and now she didn't sound so cute anymore.

"At the great hurling match between Cork and Tipperary
that was held in the park on the banks of the Lee
our own darling boys were afraid of being beaten
so they sent for Bold Thaddy in Ballinagree
well he hurled the ball left and right in their faces
he showed those Tipperary boys daring and skill
If they touched on his lines he would certainly brain them
and the papers sang praises of the Bold Thaddy Quill"

One of the men spits on the ground and then stares at Charlie. "What the fuck is this bitch singing about?"

It was clear to Charlie what the song was about. You was challenging the men and Charlie was supposed to prove her masculinity and get in a fight with them.

Charlie steps up, absolutely fucking shaking inside but staying mannish as fuck and hating You for the situation. No one likes to get in fights. Not really.

What would a macho do? A macho would tell the men not to talk to You like that.

She tells the men not to call You a bitch.

You gives her puppy eyes as encouragement. As in Charlie is her savior and needs to protect her.

"We can call her a bitch if we want to. And you're a bitch too." Grunts one of the men.

"They're calling us bitches". You is almost crying.

Charlie looks around and sees a loose brick next to some fast food wrappers. She picks up the brick, takes a deep breath and looks over her shoulder at You, hating You for forcing her to prove her masculinity. Then she stalks straight towards the men.

The entire street goes silent. All these partying buffoons, out of their wits one second. Then suddenly extremely aware that something is going down.

Charlie has almost reached the men. Her gait is stiff.

You's eyes tear up and her cute mouth turns into an evil grimace and she salivates like a dog. Someone is about to get their ass kicked and it's all for her.

"Gooood" she moans.

"Put that fucking brick down you bitch." One of the men says. They're both taller than they looked from a distance.

Whatever. Charlie smacks the first guy right in the face with the brick, breaking his nose and sending a fountain of blood right back onto her own face. The second guy tackles her to the ground. His weight crushing her ribs. He sits up on her belly and subdues her arms.

"Stop!" He shouts.

She smacks him with the brick but from this angle she barely scrapes his cheek. He grabs the brick and throws it away.

His friend is twisting and turning on the ground beside them, blood still spurting from his nose. “Fuuug, ma mowse.”

You is psychopathic. She is ecstatic. She shouts “Fuck them up! Charlie! Get up! Fuck him up!”

Charlie is confused. She can’t move though. What is she supposed to do.

The street is filled with high pitched women’s screams like sirens. Screech! And men making ape noises. Woo!

The cops arrive and so does an ambulance. Charlie looks around for You and catches a glimpse of her yellow ponytail and of her boney butt as she disappears into the crowd.

This isn’t what I wanted.

CHAPTER FOUR

It is night in the park with all the homeless guys.

There's a row of them along the pebble path that leads through the park to a tower that looks like a fairytale castle. A disturbance in the magnetosphere that has been caused by solar winds has lit the horizon in a green aurora. The green aurora sways back and forth like a wave.

Dmitry is sitting on a bench with two suitcases filled with his things. If he at least had a safe place to leave them then he could move about more freely. But like this, lugging luggage with him everywhere, he looks like a homeless guy and that's gross.

As a matter of fact, he is homeless but deep in his heart he knows that he isn't gross. Not like the real homeless guys on the other park benches. They've been homeless longer.

Dmitry is resisting the urge to call his mom. He comes from an Ukrainian Orthodox family and his mother doesn't agree with his lifestyle. She wishes her son was a man. That's the best way to put it.

He is staring at his phone, the contact "Mom" on the screen, the light from the display on his face.

He's pissed off at his mom for not loving him how he is, but deep down he wishes he could make her proud. He wants to go out and party. He is angry at Bob and at his current circumstance.

All the men along the path are incredibly still and the only thing moving is the aurora. Then an old man in tattered clothing detaches himself from the row of men and begins to walk slowly towards Dmitry.

Dmitry's heart starts beating fast the way it did when

Bob would approach. Is it anticipation or fear?

The old man comes closer slowly, like a demon on the prowl and Dmitry feels a relatively new feeling. It's one of disgust. Of being better than this man. Of hate and anger.

The man has a white beard and crazy white hair. His clothes stink. Dmitry hopes that the man will keep walking but he doesn't. He stops right in front of Dmitry and stares at him with angry blue eyes.

Dmitry squares his shoulders like a man. Like how his mother wanted him to be. He grits his jaw and looks up and asks the old man what he thinks he's looking at.

"You should live." The old man says.

Dmitry scowls and asks what the fuck that means.

"Live."

Dmitry tells the old man to fuck off. No seriously fuck off or I'll kick your ass.

Someone whistles. Shrill. A shrill whistle. A bunch of homeless men sit up on their benches and look at Dmitry. It's so creepy.

The old man seems hurt. "I was trying to give you advice."

There are many eyes on Dmitry now. The aurora has stopped swaying and just hangs in the sky like a green washcloth.

Dmitry throws his head back like a mermaid, gets up, grabs his two suitcases and stalks out of the park in the opposite direction of the castle. His butt wagging. Yas.

Dmitry has made it to the O'Gay Pub. The only gay Irish Pub in town. He knows a few people here. Like this black bartender called Snort. Snort has broad shoulders and a flabby neck. Snort gives Dmitry cocaine for free, no strings attached. He senses that Dmitry isn't doing well.

"What happened to your face?"

Dmitry's shoulders are square. He leaves his suitcases behind the bar.

Dmitry does it in a toilet stall. There's a naked man down there. Just naked with his cock and balls hanging out. Wiry, wearing some kind of harness. Dmitry is in no mood. He does the cocaine in the stall.

Whoooooooooooosh. He's a fucking butterfly!

He flaps his butt cheeks and flies up the stairs to the dance floor. The music is a bit hardcore but whatevs. He dances with aaalll the guys. Aaalll night long. The colors from the old disco lights at O'Gays are so amazeballs he writes in his review and takes a picture of this one big and hairy dark Bin Laden looking sumumabitch.

Dmitry and the Arab go upstairs to the VIP area. Snort, the black bartender looks worried. Ah he's just jealous.

In the VIP area the fairy makes out with the monster. But just a little. That's when Dmitry remembers how Bob punched him and hurt him.

Dmitry gets angry and pushes Al Qaida away. But Al Qaida doesn't quit. He keeps pushing forward.

"Oh Yeah. Fuck yeah. I like it when you play hard to get."

Dmitry tells him no but the guy pushes forward and pushes Dmitry against a wall.

"Fuck yeah suck my dick." He tries to push Dmitry down onto his knees.

Dmitry has had enough. He grabs Isis's jacket and rams his forehead right into his teeth. Ukrainian style. It's a bit racist, he knows but whatever.

The big guy goes down. Down down. And he's down for the count because Dmitry starts stomping him with his pink hiking boots.

The guy is bleeding.

A whole crowd of Gay guys rushes Dmitry and subdues him. They're all fucking over him. All those faces and arms and torsos and swinging dicks, trying to make sure that he doesn't kill anyone.

In that moment the DJ puts on a remix of "Lost Wandering Blues", sung by Ma Rainey who surely must be a real mermaid and Dmitry can't help but smile.

I‘m leavin‘ this mornin‘ with my clothes in my hand
I‘m leavin‘ this mornin‘ with my clothes in my hand
I won‘t stop movin‘ till I find my man

I‘m standin‘ here wonderin‘ will a matchbox hold my clothes?
I‘m standin‘ here wonderin‘ will a matchbox hold my clothes?
I got a trunk too big to be botherin‘ with on the road

First they call the cops and then an ambulance because Dmitry won't stop screaming about butterflies and fairies and mermaids.

Snort has gotten the fuck out of there. He doesn't know if the shit he gives people is actual cocaine or if there's more in there. He gets it from a funny looking drag queen called Miss Eternal, who has literally murdered people. So, as soon as the cops arrived, Snort fucking fled the scene.

Mohammed decides not to press charges and Dmitry is injected with something and tied to a stretcher. His tongue becomes useless and he can no longer talk about cute things.

They put him in the ambulance. Three strong nurses.

Fuuuck them. Fuuuck all of them. The doctor shines a light in his face and his nametag says “Dr. Me”.

Me seems worried. Me tells the nurses some medicinal gibberish. The nurses seem to understand Me.

“What’s your name?” Me asks, and then, “Have you taken any drugs tonight? Where are the bruises on your face from? Where do you live?”

Me is nice.

CHAPTER FIVE

I am an Eternal Boxer sitting in a spaceship, flying to Mars. I have four large bumps on my head from fights I was in. Some I won and some I lost. Each of the bumps has a face and a personality. My bumps have eyes and noses and mouths. One leers and another frowns and another laughs. One bumps mouth is another bumps eye.

I have boxing gloves for hands. Boxing gloves eternally glued to my wrists. I am reading a story on my communicator and I have to use my thumbs to swipe the pages because boxing gloves don't have fingers.

Operating my communicator this way takes a long time. But I am reading a story about two lovers who must meet and must fall in love. It is of high importance to the future of the universe that they do. One is a man who thinks he is a girl and a girl who thinks she is a guy.

The truth is that they are caught up in the major narrative of their time. Narrative is labels. And the truth is that homosexuality and heterosexuality and all kinds of sexuality are all part of the same powerful interconnected star… Love…

Someone SNEEZES!

Someone SNEEZES!

I am distracted. I can no longer think about true love.

The flight attendant slithers by and SNIFFS!

The flight attendant is an inhuman creature.

His ears are SPIRALS and his head is bald and EXPRESSIONLESS. He has no legs but a LARGE, CURVY TAIL instead!

His T-Shirt has an image of a robot on it and the robot has an image of a HEART on its chest!

This is not love! This is an ABSTRACTION!

He stares at me WIDE EYED and WIDE MOUTHED and I forget the faces of the people I love. The people I miss. The woman and the man and the child. I forget their faces…

He SNIFFS again…

I bring the boxing gloves up towards my face to shield myself from this invasion and the flight attendant MIMICS me!

Categorizing love is a crime against nature. I have better things to do than to deal with this assault.

I am an Eternal Boxer sitting in a spaceship on my way to a boxing match on Mars which I must win! I MUST WIN!

They do this. The flight attendants on my way to fights. They watch me and profile me. They distract me and take my thoughts away. When I think something positive they will put a negative into my mind. And when I think something negative they will adjust with a positive. When I think about a woman a man will make a noise and when

I think about a man a woman will make a noise. But I need to read this story about this man who believes that he is a woman and this woman who believes that she is a man.

IT'S TORTURE!

I drop my gloves and the flight attendant slithers on down the aisle past the other passengers.

I look out the window at the streaks of stars rushing by and I see my own reflection. The bumps on my head are in despair. Some hysterical, others in agony. The eyes on my own face have dark circles around them.

I believe that I carry a little bit of every human being inside of me. It's true. I may understand the soldier, shooting off his enemy's head out of revenge because I once ripped the head off an ant that bit me. Or maybe because my ancestors used revenge against a rival clan and were successful. It's the same with every person. There's a relatable aspect to everyone. People need to understand that about storytelling. I am reading a story about these two lovers but I am still me. Growing up means choosing your identity. But that's bullshit. In the end I am everyone and everyone is me. When regarding the core aspects of our existence of course. Even animals are relatable. Our brainstem is the same. A crocodile fetus and a human fetus are identical in the first few stages of development.

In the window I see the reflection of the flight attendant slithering along the aisle back towards me again. He's about to SNIFF! I know it. I am sure that I am being profiled. They think that I'm some sort of monster, so they are not allowing me to have deep thoughts.

I shut my eyes and wait for him to pass. I need to get to the boxing match on mars.

SNORT!

And I need to read this story about these two lovers, so I gather my thoughts and keep swiping painstakingly with my thumbs.

CHAPTER SIX

The guy she hit on the head with a brick presses charges and Charlie goes to court. She feels naked. She used to fly amongst the stars and now she's crashing down towards earth, totally exposed.

She's careful now. Very careful so as not to make anymore mistakes while the court case is going on. She takes one careful step at a time. She writes her former business partners in a quiet tone, hoping to be hired for a new project. She goes to the supermarket to buy just a few things. Nothing expensive and nothing extravagant.

The speed test could come at any time. She doesn't drive but the speed test is proverbial. Maybe the speed test could be her former boss, seeing her splurge on expensive wine at the market. Maybe the speed test could be Tammy, seeing Charlie happy around town and then Tammy would get mad and ruin her reputation. The speed test could be Charlie getting in an argument with another rude guy and the cops intervene again and then she would definitely go to jail.

In court things are tense and You is nowhere to be seen. She became a ghost when she removed herself from the scene. Charlie shouldn't have trusted a girl she barely knew.

Luckily the Jury seems woke. It's made up of an extravagant group of animals. Peacocks, Lions, and Dragonflies. Charlie is biding her time and using her powers of foresight to predict a miracle, which sometimes works. At times, the courtroom seems almost idyllic.

The guy she hit in the face with a brick has a wife and a

2 year old son who climbs all over his dad every chance he gets. Seeing this makes Charlie actually feel bad about what she did. It also makes her nipples tingle and her uterus feel like an empty cave.

When it's Charlie's turn to give her statement she cries and apologizes. Both the tears and the apology are real. The man with the broken face replies "I forgive you for the sake of my son. I want him to learn that forgiveness is the answer and violence is not." There's a snake-like quality to his speech and it is obvious that his jaw hurts. His wife glares at Charlie as if she wants to shank her.

Charlie is given an option. 5 months in Jail and 500 hours of community service or 9 months in a mental institution to treat her aggression. Without hesitation she and her lawyer decide that she will go to the mental institution.

Charlie has private health insurance and will be treated like a queen there.

Charlie is falling past the stars and through yellow and blue and red nebulas and has almost reached earth. She asks herself if she will land in the sea, or on a mountain-top or in a valley. Will it be warm or cold? Will there be fire or ice?

Her falling speed increases more and more and she falls faster and faster.

CHAPTER SEVEN

They put Dmitry on really strong meds. These calm him down, make him think less, and make him more aware of himself. They take his phone away and in its absence from his life, he realizes that the phone was a false reflection of himself. All the mermaids and butterflies were a false likeness.

His true portrait is different. He looks at himself in the mirror now. He is a handsome man with a heart-shaped head and with broad shoulders. He is a bit fat around the waist and the rump but whatever. He lets his beard grow out. It is ginger. He looks in the bathroom mirror and considers himself a bear.

Because of the severity of his condition, he can't leave the station for another two weeks. He looks out the window at the garden, which is a nice green and wishes that he could stroll around in it. The weather is nice and he would like to touch a leaf or a tree. So far his summer hasn't been so great and he would like to enjoy the last part of it.

Dmitry develops clinomania. An excessive desire to stay in bed. Sometimes one of the other patients will knock on his door and ask if he wants to play a board game. Or a bored game as Dmitry sees it. Boring.

Sometimes he will say yes and play cards for a few hours and sometimes he will say no and stay in bed. Bye bye boring.

Without any money in his pocket he can't buy anything from the little store by the hospital entrance either and so he is forced to eat the mud that they give the patients that have government health insurance.

The patients that have private insurance get their own table. And they get food that is mouthwatering to look at. Like sushi or hamburgers. Dmitry is jealous, but at least he's losing some of the weight around his ass.

He also doesn't get to see the head doctor. Instead is treated by the second tier.

The doctors study him. They take him apart in therapy. And the other patients too. And then they try to figure out ways to put them all together again.

And when the patients all sit together at lunch they do the same with each other. They study each other. Try to understand each other's internal organs.

Dmitry starts to draw. But not butterflies and unicorns. He draws the other patients. The ones who have been lobotomized and drool. The ones with paper crowns. He figures that looking special can make you special and being special can make you look special.

He draws an old couple nude. A woman and a man. They are patients and have agreed to be his subjects. He studies their form. He abstracts it into the different parts of the body. The eyes, the mouth, the arms, the bones, the heart and liver and nose. They are sooo old and wrinkly. Her vagina isn't very pretty. Her breasts are just flaps. His balls hang really low and he has hair on his shoulders but not his head. But they have been together for a long time. Dmitry tears up a little.

He tries to understand the relationship between the parts and the whole the way the doctors do. He realizes that he had been opened up before he came here. He had been shattered into multiple pieces when Bob punched him. Pink and blue cute fairytale animals.

He realizes that being opened up for everyone to analyze was unhealthy and that he needs to put up walls in order to stay sane. Being open for too long is painful.

He finally calls his mom. He remembers the phone number because it hasn't changed since he was a child.

Bleep…
Bleep…
Bleep…

"Hello?" His mom's voice makes his heart flutter and he hates her for it.

He tells her where he is.

"Oh dear Lord. Why don't you ever listen to me? I told you that all this gayness would end badly."

He sighs and considers what she said. He tells her that in a way she is right. He's had enough of men. And done with sex and done with perversion.

"Oh my baby. Tell me everything that happened."

He tells her the whole story, about Bob hitting him and kicking him out and about becoming homeless and about what happened at the O'Gay bar.

"Oh baby please pray to Jesus tonight. Please."

He tells her that he will.

"Should I come visit you?"

He tells her no and that she should save the money for the trip and wire it to him because he is broke.

"Yes baby, of course. I will send you some money right away. You know that I still have faith in you baby?"

Yes Dmitry knows. He says goodbye.

"Bye baby. I'll talk to you soon."

Dmitry hangs up the phone.

Dmitry turns around and sees something that truly makes his heart melt and his mouth widen and his eyes too.

A girl is brought in past the entrance to the psych ward. She looks disheveled but so innocent. Like a woodland fairytale creature that has lost her wings and fallen from her tree. Her face is boyish but her lips so feminine and a natural pink. Her hands so small and her waist so slim. She is the most pretty little thing he has ever seen in real life.

He quickly averts his gaze and hides behind a corner and begins to overhear. The girl is speaking to Dr. Me, the psychiatrist that first brought Dmitry to the hospital.

"I'm Dr. Me. What is your name?"

The girl answers "My name is Charlie." And her voice is tough and steady.

Dmitry repeats Charlie in his head. Charlie. What a masculine fucking name. She's got it all.

Dmitry gets giddy in a good way.

CHAPTER EIGHT

I'm standing in a boxing ring in the Valles Marineris, the largest canyon in the solar system. It is 3000 kilometers long, 600 km across and is 8 kilometers deep.

Most sports events on Mars take place somewhere along this canyon which makes the Grand Canyon back on earth seem like a crack in the ground.

The arena is in the shape of an inverted pyramid. The red canyon walls have been converted into seats for the visitors. There are about 300,000,000 present for this match.

The boxing ring has anti gravity boosters that make it float around the canyon in order to give every visitor a chance to see the action with their own eyes. There are of course also multiple large screens which allow the guests to follow the fight in detail.

As a boxer, I'm a big deal and so is my opponent.

My opponents name is Alex and Claire. One body that houses two people. The right side is masculine with gigantic muscles and a handsome male head called Alex and the left side is Claire, a beautiful toned yet soft model of a woman with long red hair.

Nobody really knows where Alex and Claire came from. Some say that they are brother and sister, however there is evidence in the tabloid magazines that suggests that they are lovers who loved each other so much that they melded their bodies together.

I raise my eternal boxing gloves above my head. The

ones that have been welded to my wrists for all infinity and the crowd goes wild. They know my record and my story. That I hardly ever lose a fight and that I'm being profiled and harassed by the bald snake people with spiral ears who don't allow me to think beautiful thoughts.

A short promotional video about myself plays on the big screen with images of me shadow boxing while listening to songs by Ma Rainey. The faces on my head all sing along.

Then footage of my last fight plays. It was against a goliath called Tim. I got hit on the head and a new face appeared like a bump and leered idiotically.

The video ends with the question of how many new bumps I will receive on my scalp today or whether I can avoid the abuse.

Then a video plays about Alex and Claire. Their motivational music is Claire de Lune by Debussy. It shows knockout after knockout. Claire jabbing jabbing jabbing at the opponent with beauty and grace and then, just at the right moment Alex delivering a brutal right. Bam bam bam. One opponent after another goes down.

The purse for this fight is a real golden statue of a family. A father a mother and a child. All embracing each other. It stands on a floating pedestal for now, until the winner of the fight has been decided. It glows warm and makes me smell honey and cinnamon. And it draws tears into my tear-ducts and the bags under my eyes get heavy heavy. I really want to win this statue of the family. I really want it.

And all of a sudden the bell tolls and the crowd erupts in cheer and the fight has begun.

Alex and Claire come out aggressive and I hold back. Claire jabs jabs jabs. I throw a jab at her which misses and Alex goes for his knockout straight. But I anticipate it and duck.

And Claire goes again, jab jab jab. This time I weave and throw Alex a right hook. Claire's next jab hits me on the right side of my face and my hook barely connects with Alex.

I try to figure out their rhythm and a way in. I crouch and try to go for a left hook to Alex's side of the body. Both Alex and Claire hit me on the top of the head with a flurry of hooks. The faces on my scalp jiggle and scream and yelp in pain and I shrink back.

They are pushing me backwards towards the ropes. The cheering of the crowd is muted and I am the Eternal Boxer.

We throw jabs and punches back and forth. Alex and Claire lead the dance and I dodge.

The rhythm…

It's Claire de Lune…

I hear my chance and I change a note. Claire is a jab jab jabbing and I duck and weave to the right and throw a right hook at Claire's head…

It connects, wham! Her head sways to the side and her

leg wobbles and she drops. Alex goes down onto one knee and pushes his fist into the floor in order to counterbalance Claire's ragdoll weight.

The entire inverted pyramid erupts in ecstatic applause. The Eternal Boxer has landed the first knockdown.

Alex and Claire slowly get up and we go at it again for another few seconds but I don't land another knockdown.

The bell rings, ding ding and I go back to my corner and Alex and Claire go back to theirs.

I'm in good shape. My corner man massages the faces on my head. Their tongues loll happily.

I stare at the golden statue of the family, up on its floating pedestal. If I win this fight I win much more than the golden statue of the family. I win my freedom. I will never be profiled by the snake people again. I will finally be allowed to be happy. I will no longer be a deviant. I will be a hero.

And ding ding the next round begins.

I come out swinging this time. I'm sure of myself and of the rhythm. Alex and Claire are more careful than they were before. I go for the same tactic again. I'm too sure of myself.

I feel the rhythm and let Claire jab jab jab and I duck and sway to the right and send her a right hook…

Which misses because in that moment Alex SNIFFS!

He SNIFFS!

How does he know to SNIFF? Who told him to SNIFF? Who told him my weakness? Is the fight rigged?

I see the right hook heading towards me as if in slow motion and I know that this will hurt. The faces on my head screech!

Whaam. It connects and I see stars as I spin to the floor like a dreidel and a new bump immediately appears on my head and with it a new face.

The new face doesn't know what's going in and decides to first greet the other faces. "Oh hi!"

The other faces greet it back. "Hi friend! We hang out on this guys head and we're in a fight right now."

As the faces continue talking to each other the count-down begins. The 300,000,000 audience members chant the count down. I fight against the floor and try to push myself back up.

"10!"

Nope not getting up.

"9!"

It's as if I'm trying to drive the floor down. And this boxing ring is heavy.

"8!"

Is a good number, like an upright infinity sign… I'm on my knees.

"7!"

Was a magical number in Ancient Egypt. It combined the heavenly with the worldly.

"6!"

Some of the bumps on my head have joined in the chanting. Idiots.

"5!"

A few bumps are trying to motivate me to get up. "You can do it!"

"4!"

Is the number that represented the worldly in ancient Egypt. Like the four corners of the pyramid.

"3!"

Represented the heavenly, like the triangle sides of the pyramid which point towards the sky.

"2!"

And I'm up!
Ding ding!

I stagger into my corner. My bumps are blabbering uncontrollably. That was a hard fucking hit. I need some quiet to think. I tell them to shut the fuck up and they do.

I figure everything in life is like an inverted pyramid. It's how ideas progress. You start with one idea such as how to make fire, and next you have two more ideas, you can cook meat or boil water, and after that four more ideas, stew, tea, vodka, and smoked fish. This goes all the way up to spaceships and anti-gravity boxing rings. The brain is like that too. At the bottom you have the brainstem then the cerebellum and then the cerebrum at the top. The instincts at the bottom, the unconscious mind in the middle and the conscious mind at the top. It's the same for any organization too. You have the CEO and then the board of directors and then the different departments.

I stare at the prize up on its pedestal. A golden statue of a happy family.

Ding ding, the third round begins and I'm determined.

Alex and Claire step up and start throwing punches, hoping to capitalize off of the last knockdown they landed on me. I no longer give a fuck. I copy the Claire de Lune and anticipate their punches and in doing so suddenly I am able to anticipate their SNIFFS.

SNIFF! That was Claire.

SNIFF! That was Alex.
Now I'm fucking angry.
SNIFF! That was me and I follow with a flurry of pun-

ches and break their rhythm once and for all.

I bob and weave, throw a lead hook at Alex, a right hook at Claire, a lead uppercut at Alex, a lead uppercut at Claire and a rear cross overhand that hits first Claire on the jaw and then Alex.

They go down like wobbly-heads and the pyramid explodes.

Fireworks are shot into the sky and the sound of millions of Beedeeboos makes the 3000 kilometers of Valles Marineris canyon shake. Beedeeboos are the Martian version of a Vuvuzela.

There is no way that Alex and Claire are getting up again. They look like a squid on land.

Confetti rains down on me and two cherubs with little golden wings pick me up by my shoulders and fly me towards the pedestal with the golden statue of the man the woman and the child on it.

The giant screens broadcast my floating, grinning face as I get closer and closer to the prize. The faces on my head are having a party. Party hats and blowers.

Some screens are showing my brilliant combination and double knockout in a loop and every time it lands there are more cheers.

I stretch out my eternal boxing glove hands towards the statue which turns out to be life sized. I anticipate hugging it with all my being…

The cherubs have carried me close.

And then I'm there and they drop me down right next to the golden family. I hug them all. The mother, the father and the child. I hug them and I cry.

I cry.

My large tear ducts finally able to empty and my eyes now shiny and round.

My bumpy head pressed against theirs one by one. I kiss them each on the forehead.

Oh how I wish they could hug me back.

CHAPTER NINE

Charlie is in her private room at the psych ward. It's nice like a cheap hotel. There's chairs and a desk and a hospital bed with a nightstand. On the wall next to her bed there's a painting of an African forest with antelopes and giraffes and lions. This is where she has landed.

Outside her window she sees a sequoia tree like the one in the backyard of her apartment.

"Breathe baby. Just breathe" Her dad tells her over the phone. Only her dad is allowed to call her Baby.

She doesn't have a lot of credit left, as she had to cancel her plan and is now paying by the minute.

"We'll talk until your credit runs out."

She starts to cry. The head doctor has put her on really strong meds. She feels like she's been reduced to a nonentity. She has been blacklisted in the film industry for not meeting her deadline.

"Just remember the good times. Don't focus on the bad." Her dad is the wisest man she knows.

Everything was going great two years ago but then she didn't find the right people to work with. Instead she fell into the wrong hands.

"I believe you, but there's nothing you can do about that now. You're in the situation that you're in." Her dad replies.

Yes, but things should have been different. She is really good at what she does. It isn't fair that she shouldn't be able to pursue her career and that she's in the psych ward instead.

"You hit that man with a brick. He forgave you. This is you being let off lightly." Charlie gasps. Streaks of saliva hang from her teeth. Her nose is running and her eyes and cheeks are wet. She wishes she was a little girl again, in her dad's arms. He was so big like a tree and she was so small.

"Baby I wish that too. But you're an adult now and you have to deal with the consequences of your actions."

She says goodbye.

"Goodbye baby. Send me a text anytime and I'll call you back."

Charlie stares out the window at the sequoia and then her drugged gaze drifts around the garden. She remembers the last time she saw Tammy. In her pink superhero cape. Disappearing into the distance past the sequoia in their backyard.

She misses Tammy in her bones.

Charlie remembers that crazy night with You. The night You made her hit that man in the head and then You disappeared. The reason Charlie is here now. She hates You for what happened.

She stares at her phone. No messages from work. Nothing to coordinate. Her hand shakes as if she was an alcoholic in remission.

A speaker that hangs from the wall beeps and Dr. Me says. "To all patients. Group therapy in the dining hall has begun"

Group therapy consists of all the patients sitting on chairs in a circle and talking about themselves. Anything really. Dr. Me moderates.

The patients are all strange but the creepiest of all is this big ginger guy who introduces himself "Hi I'm Dmitry."

His full beard makes him look overly masculine, yet his eyes are soft. He keeps staring at Charlie with an open mouth and when Charlie looks back at him he averts his gaze. Charlie doesn't like this kind of attention, especially not from men.

There's a woman who looks like a mental patient from the 1950s. She has a large scar on her head and her body is deformed. She can't speak properly. "I was cooking on the week. It was good. End." She says.

A wiry little man wearing a paper crown who has a black eye and multiple scratches all over his body talks about his sleep-walking issues. "I wake up like this. The day before there was nothing but today I have a black eye. Lock your doors at night, I've been known to steal things in my sleep."

There's a beautiful old couple holding hands. Charlie deduces that the woman is the patient and that her husband has come to visit. "We spent the day walking around the garden and enjoying the summer flowers." He says. "We saw birds and a squirrel." She almost whispers and hugs her husband.

But then it's Dmitry's turn to speak. He looks up at her, wide eyed and with a slack jaw. Then he looks around at the group. He speaks with a voice that seems too deep for his personality. Like a croak. As if he is hiding a higher pitch. "Hi. I had a nice weekend. I slept really well and I drew a few objects and people around the ward. I still haven't seen the head doctor. I would really like to. And I'd like to go walk around the garden." He looks at Charlie again and then away.

Charlie shivers but decides to stay rational. She attempts to analyze her negative reaction to him. The vibration of his voice makes her ass hurt. His stupid stare makes her feel that she is the focus of the room. His shoulders make her feel small and weak. All of it together makes her heart thud harder and that makes her angry.

Then it's her turn. She introduces herself but immediately becomes self conscious about her own voice. Her pitch has become higher! Maybe in response to the big creepy guy's croak. She pulls herself together and complains that the meds the doctors gave her are too strong and that she would also like to see the head doctor. She reminds the nurse that she is a private patient and should be treated well. Dr. Me nods and makes a note.

Dmitry stares at her and grins, wide-eyed, and then shows her his profile and runs his fingers through his beard and then his hair.

What a fucking weirdo.

Charlie spends the rest of the day alone in the dining room, watching the other patients come in and make themselves coffee or tea or eat a piece of cake and then leave. There don't seem to be any cute girls around. Only older women and all of them seem to have major psychological issues.

Dmitry pokes his head around the corner and grins, then disappears again.

Charlie sighs.

For dinner Charlie gets goulash with pasta. She is seated at a table with the other privately insured patents. The food doesn't taste too bad. The woman with the large scar on her head is sitting next to Charlie and this makes her a bit queezy. But she's seated far away from Dmitry and that is a relief.

In the evening she takes a loong shower.

At night she lies awake in bed a few moments too long. But then she falls asleep.

In the middle of the night the man with the paper crown and the black eye and the scratches walks into her room and scares a screech out of her. He doesn't seem to notice. He runs around the room like a maniac, bumping into things. He grabs Charlie's toothbrush and bunny hops out of the room.

Charlie gets up and complains to the nurse that's on the graveyard shift. The nurse HOOTS and squeals. "I'm dead!" And then she goes to the old man's room and retrieves Charlie's toothbrush for her.

Charlie washes the toothbrush thoroughly, shoves her nightstand in front of the door and then goes to bed again. She lies awake a few moments too long. But then she falls asleep and doesn't wake up until the morning.

CHAPTER TEN

Dmitry is standing in line to receive his meds from the nurses. But there's a couple of patients ahead of Dmitry and Dmitry hates waiting. He looks around bored and catches a glimpse of Charlie as she rounds a corner, her shoulders sagging. She gets in line behind him and avoids eye contact.

She's so cute he could melt.

A nurse SNIFFS.

Instead of melting Dmitry lifts his shoulders and pushes out his jaw because he's trying to be more masculine.

He's gotten quite accustomed to the meds and the calming effect that they have on him so he's looking forward to taking them. There's one in particular that he likes. It's small and white and dissolves on the tongue.

It's Dmitry's turn and as one nurse measures his blood pressure the other gives him his pill salad which he washes down with a glass of water. In the manliest voice he can muster he asks the salad nurse if they can make an exception and let him leave for 15 minutes to go to the little store at the hospital entrance.

"Yes I think that'll be alright. But no longer than that." The nurse replies.

He smiles and thanks the nurses, then flashes Charlie a handsome grin and leaves the ward.

There's an ATM at the store and he withdraws the money that his mom transferred to his account. He doesn't spend it all but he does binge. He eats five donuts in a row, each with a different color frosting. Pink, blue, green, yellow, and red. Then he gets a slurpee in the most giant cup and fills it with Pink, blue, green, yellow and red flavor.

The 15 minutes are up and he's bloated. He draws in his stomach and struts back to the ward and to Yoga Therapy which is coming up.

CHAPTER ELEVEN

Charlie has Yoga therapy. She is one of the first to arrive. The floor of the room is covered in blue mats. Long drawn female vocals emanate from a small speaker and flow around the room. The instructor is an Indian man with a curly black beard who is already in Sukhasana pose with a straight spine and googly eyes staring at the tip of his nose.

"Please take off your shoes and then take a seat anywhere." He motions towards the mats.

So she removes her shoes and then picks a mat in a far corner. This way she will have a patient on her left and a wall on her right. She doesn't want to feel surrounded.

The other patients enter and pick mats and are quiet out of respect for the atmosphere. Charlie knows this effect from her work. Everything has a context, and when people understand the context they will behave accordingly automatically. The context in this room is silence and respect.

Dmitry, the big ginger guy, enters last and grins at her and then picks the last mat that is left, which is on the opposite side of the room.

She sighs.

The guru turns off the music. "Please take the pose that you see me taking." He instructs. "Now cross your forearms below the wrists in front of your chest and chant together with me."

Charlie and the other patients do their best to copy the posture.

Then he begins to chant. “Sa-ta-na-ma”. In repetition and the patients join in.

Charlie notices that the chanting has become a loop in her mind and in her chest. Her breathing is becoming more and more circular. She is feeling it.

Then suddenly the guru SNIFFS!

Charlie is shocked by the sharpness of the noise and looks up. She has suddenly been taken completely out of the trance. Out of the context.

She looks around. The guru and the other patients still have their eyes fixed firmly on the tips of their noses and are still chanting “Sa-ta-na-ma”.

No one else seemed to notice the invasiveness of the SNIFF.

Except for Dmitry.

His face is ruby red with anger at having being taken out of the trance. But when he turns his head towards Charlie and his eyes recognize her face he immediately relaxes again.

She wonders what his deal is. Did she just calm him down with a glance?

The guru speaks to the group. “Now please as you say Sa, you touch the tip of your thumbs to your index fingers. At Ta you touch the tips of the thumbs to the middle fingers. At Na you touch the tip of the thumbs to the ring fingers and at Ma you touch the tip of the thumbs to the pinky fingers.”

Dmitry squares his shoulders, turns towards the guru and does as told. Charlie looks down at her hands and also follows the directions. It takes her a few tries until her thinker and her fingers are back in the loop.

CHAPTER TWELVE

A group of patients led by a physiotherapist are on a walk in the garden. Dmitry and Charlie are there too. Charlie is trailing behind and Dmitry is at the front of the group.

The garden is lush and green and the sprinklers are on. A gardener who is working on a bed of pink flowers smiles at Dmitry and nods and Dmitry nods back.

There are flowers in the trees too. White ones. And the branches look like lungs. Dmitry thinks they are lungs. They breathe in carbon dioxide and he breathes out carbon dioxide. They breathe out oxygen and he breathes in oxygen.

Then the gardener SNIFFS!

Dmitry drops his thoughts and his head. He looks back over his shoulder at Charlie.

Charlie seems also to have been taken out of her train of thought by the noise. She is looking at her feet. Her body a pretty little shape.

He wonders why he finds her so endearing. Why does she make his heart beat faster. To see a princess outside of himself? Is that what it is? A real one right there outside of his brain. A mermaid and a fairy.

He's noticed that she doesn't dress girly. He wonders if she is gay as well. He has been wanting to speak with her for a while but hasn't been able to assemble the courage.

He falls behind and starts walking next to her. She looks up at him and smiles.

"Hi I'm Dmitry."
"I know."
"And you're Charlie."
"I know that too." Charlie smiles.

Charlie wonders why he makes her heart beat fast. This is how it works. Out of fear and out of joy and out of necessity and out of wanting comfort and all of it together. Maybe they can be friends despite their differences.

Maybe they can touch someday…

She shakes that thought out of her head.

The gardener wipes his nose with his sleeve like some kind of angel. This is how it goes.

CHAPTER THIRTEEN

Dmitry and Charlie are hanging out in Dmitry's room. He has pencil drawings of the other patients plastered all over his walls. Charlie thinks that she hadn't pegged him for an artist. Rather some tough ginger idiot.

The drawing of the woman with the scar on her head, as if she had been lobotomized is beautiful. He has accentuated her beauty. Her lips and her large eyes.

Charlie strokes her own cheek.

The drawing of the man with the paper crown, who raids other people's rooms at night in nothing but his underwear is hilarious. Dmitry has given him a jetpack and a tightrope to walk on.

Charlie can't help but laugh.

The old couple in the nude… Love eternal. Just that. Wrinkly and true love eternal. It exists here in these thick and wobbly pencil strokes. In the representation of the reality of a couple where both have kept love for the other through all.

Dmitry is drawing Charlie now without having asked if he could. Normally Charlie would have her defenses up, but with all this truth and loveliness she feels exceptional.

"Are you gay?"

"Yes I am."
"So am I."

"Awesome."

They both smile.

"Why are you here?"

"I went nuts."

"Did you hurt someone?"

"Yes."

"Me too."

They look at each other with understanding.

"Why did you?"

"Lost my partner and went extra."

"Same."

"Really?"

"Yeah."

"This is hilarious."

"We are the same person."

"This conversation could have totally gone the other way around as well and it would have still had the same outcome."

"Yup."

Dmitry can't seem to get Charlie's lips right. The most beautiful part. He uses an eraser and goes again."

"Ok so how are we different?"

"Well I'm female and you're male."

"I have a beard and you don't."

"And you're ginger and I have brown hair."

"Where do you wish you could go if you weren't here?"

"Africa. To see the animals. I've always wanted that. You?"

"Disneyland."

They laugh together. Together.

Dmitry flicks a few more strokes across the paper and then shows Charlie the drawing. He has brought her lips and her breasts and her hips to the foreground. Charlie thinks it makes her look like a pornstar.

She is outraged. "You made me more feminine!" Her voice high pitched and girly by mistake.

"And you make me more masculine." Dmitry growls back at her like an African lion.

CHAPTER FOURTEEN

Dmitry is sitting in the garden, anxiously or perhaps angrily balling his fists. He's waiting for a visit from Bob. Bob that fucking asshole that punched him in the face and threw him out onto his pink booty shorts.

Bob asked for an audience. He probably wants to apologize.

When Dmitry got dressed this morning he avoided wearing pink or anything too cute for that matter. He wants Bob to respect him. He's got a plan. He's going to tell Bob off.

Dmitry sees some movement out of the corner of his eye. Could this be Bob? He casually turns his head. No it's not Bob. It's a nurse rounding a corner. And she's gone. Dmitry looks down at the ground and notices something.

Fuck my life.

He's wearing his pink hiking boots. Too feminine. He didn't even notice when he put them on. But then again these are the boots he used to stomp that middle-eastern guy. So they're powerful boots.

Maybe Bob will get a stomping too. But that would mean jail. So no. But he'll tell him off for sure.

There's movement out of the corner of his eye. Could this be Bob? He casually turns his head.

Yup it's Bob. Dmitry feels blood rushing to his head. This is anger.

Bob's broad frame. His wide and wiry shoulders and long hairy arms. His hairy face. His old man strength.

His fist that hurts when it cracks your face and his brown fingertips from the crack he does. Bob is ambling down the path and he definitely doesn't fit in with the flowers and the butterflies.

Bob looks up from the path. When he sees Dmitry he stops scowling and tries to look handsome instead. The balls on this dick.

Dmitry stops himself mid eye roll.

"Hey Dmitry." Bob widens his arms as if to hug Dmitry.

But Dmitry holds out his hand for a handshake. Bob looks down at the hand, confused but then takes it.

Dmitry notices that he is still scared of Bob. So he deepens his voice and says hi back.

Bob nods. "Thanks for letting me see you."

Dmitry asks him what he wants.

"I want to apologize." Bob tries to look like James Dean by glancing down at his feet, and then flashing his dark eyes up at Dmitry.

Dmitry straight up tells Bob that the apology is not accepted.

Bob scowls. "What?"

Dmitry tells him that he heard him correct and that he should maybe check his ears if he can't hear words spoken at a normal tone.

“No I heard you… but why won’t you accept my apology...” Bob’s voice is faltering.

Dmitry tells him that what he did he can go do to someone else and that Dmitry has too much self respect to put up with that kind of treatment. Dmitry is a real snag and really masculine and Bob should not have beaten him and kicked him out. And if he ever tried something like that again Dmitry would stomp him with his pink boots. Yes Bob you heard that right. Stomped with pink fucking boots.

This time Bob takes a step back. He looks at Dmitry’s boots and then up at Dmitry’s determined face. Dmitry raises his eyebrows.

Bob probes. “Why the fuck do you have a beard? You looked so pretty before.”

Pretty? How dare Bob call him pretty. Dmitry is much more of a man than Bob will ever ever be. Bob is nothing he films shitty landscape shots that any college student can film better with their cell-phones nowadays. Plus Bob is a FUCKING CRACKHEAD! YOU CAN’T EVEN WALK NORMALLY ANYMORE! GET THE FUCK OUT OF MY LIFE!

Bob’s breathing becomes quick and shallow. He is scared and takes a few steps back and then looks around the garden. Not at the flowers and the green but in order to see if anyone witnessed his humiliation.

SNIFF!

In that moment, the gardener steps out of a bush that's shaped like a heart and nods at Dmitry. Dmitry smiles and nods back.

Bob flinches. "Who the fuck is that?"

Dmitry tells him that it's his new boyfriend and Bob should stop being such a snoop and get the fuck out of here already he never wants to see him again.

Bob nods. "Ok. I'm sorry about what happened. Ok? Have a great life."

Bob is actually so scared that he jogs backwards a few steps before he turns around and scampers off towards the exit.

The gardener crouches down by a bed of pink flowers and tends to them as if nothing happened.

Dmitry allows himself to breathe. It's as if he's just run a marathon and his breath explodes from his lungs. He puts his hands on his knees and wheezes and pants and then he cries. No he bawls.

His tears hit the cobblestones that make up the path which leads around the garden. He tries not to make too much of a fuss and suppresses his wailing noise.

CHAPTER FIFTEEN

Tammy and You. Tammy and You. Sitting across from Charlie at a table near the entrance to the psych ward. Who would have thunk it. Tammy and You know each other. With their blonde ponytails and baby blue and pink clothing style. The two teenies in a clique together.

It was all a fucking setup. Tammy was pissed at Charlie for… for what actually? For losing her biggest client? That is no fucking reason to leave someone. And to hold a grudge and set a trap using You… that is fucking low.

You did her job well. She got Charlie all shook and then got her in a fight with two big men in order to prove her masculinity. Oh fuck that's fucking looow.

But Charlie has a plan of how to deal with this situation. Charlie puckers her lovely lips. She's much more beautiful than either of the teens anyways. They both swallow heavily in unison.

Charlie blinks her big doe eyes and smiles. The teenies jaws drop.

Tammy has something to say but is having a hard time. "I… uhm. We came here to tell you that we set you up for what you did to me."

You nods.

Charlie asks what exactly she did to her.

"You were rough with me. You pushed me off the couch and you wouldn't give me my allowance anymore."

Charlie scoffs. Then catches herself, and puckers her lips again. She calls Tammy a gold digger.

"Hey that's rude." This time it's You that's speaking.

Charlie assures them that it's not rude at all. That it's the truth. That any normal person would stand by the one they love through thick and thin and that furthermore, both of them are horrible terrible people who, in her time of need, got her involved in a fight and legal problems which ended up with her being here.

"Yes we know that." Says You.

Charlie bites her thumb in a sexy way.

Tammy's eyes begin to water. Something has gotten through to her.

Charlie continues like a queen. She tells them that she doesn't want to be here, but that at least here she has met some good people. Tammy and You may be cute on the outside but inside they are rotten.

Tammy starts bawling and hugs You.

"See what you have done?" You says. "Now she's crying."

Charlie scoffs again and this time allows them to notice. They need as much ridicule as she can give them. It may even help them in the future.

Charlie tells them that she should be crying and so should You. Charlie was in a time of real NEED. She needed SUPPORT and LOVE, a real PARTNER, not some childish bullshit. Some badly drawn hentai caricature. And as far as You is concerned, who are you anyways? A carbon copy of Tammy? Some chicken-headed, bony little shell with no soul.

Once Charlie is done she leans forward revealing her boobage.

You stares at Charlie's superior chest and then starts crying as well. "hstop..." She whispers.

What is Charlie supposed to stop? She's not doing anything. Just exposing that both Tammy and You have no sense of morals or true friendship and that they probably secretly hate each other too. The only way they can exist is by competing with one another and they would gladly stab each other in the back if they could.

You lets out a wail. Now both the girls are bawling. With snot spittle. They really do look like hentai characters. Little hentai mice. They clasp each other and their tongues lol out.

Charlie is calm and serene. She tells them honeys that they still have a lot to learn about life and that she wishes them well in their future endeavors but that they should stop contacting her please.

She has better things to do.

Tammy can't anymore "Why. Would. You. Say theeese thiiings?"

Charlie replies that obviously what she said is true otherwise they wouldn't be crying. This hits them hard.

"STOP MANSPLAINING TO US!"

Charlie laughs heartily and can't stop. No really, she can't.

"We're leaving. Come on!" You gets up and pulls at Tammy's arm.

You is pulling Tammy towards the psych ward entrance where Dr. Me is already waiting to open the door for them.

SNIFF!

The girls are jolted by the sound.

As they exit, clasping each other, the skinny little tramps, Tammy turns around one more time and makes eye contact with Charlie and whispers the words "Ih hlove hyou."

Charlie HOOTS with such ecstasy that she almost falls off her chair. But she composes herself in the last moment and holds her nose up high.

CHAPTER SIXTEEN

Dmitry is eating at the table for the government insured patients. Charlie walks in, smiles at him and then sits down with him. The other government insured patients look at her with awe. The patients at the privately insured table begin to murmur about her.
"Like in highschool." Whispers Dmitry.

"Yes they don't tell you that adults behave this way too."

"They should devote a class to it. How not to be an exclusionist pig once you're an adult."

Dmitry and Charlie high-five.

Charlie has sushi and Dmitry eyes it and licks his lips.

"Listen." Says Charlie. "I've thought about it. What if billionaires have been guiding us our whole lives so that we would get to exactly this point?"

"Well I'd say you need a higher dosage of your meds." Dmitry chuckles and drifts his gaze back to the sushi.

"No I'm serious. Just hear me out. If it's crazy it's crazy. It's just a theory ok? So, it would make sense to me that we are part of some kind of experiment. Because we're special, as in we are intelligent and unique and strong and beautiful etc. Right?"
Dmitry doesn't hesitate. "Of course we are. And handsome."

"And handsome. So what if someone has been pulling the strings and is working on something really big for us? Something this is all leading towards? It doesn't have to be a billionaire. It could be someone else. Like God."

Dmitry pulls a grimace. "Nah. I don't think so."

Charlie pushes her plate towards Dmitry. "Do you want a tuna roll?"

"Sure." He grabs one and wolfs it down. "Damn that's good."

The other government insured patients look jealous. The sleepwalker with the paper crown looks legitimately hurt at the fact that he doesn't have sushi.

Dmitry ignores him and continues. "You lost me at God. You sound like my mother."

"Ok. So how about fate?"
He shrugs. "Hm. Maybe."

"You'll say maybe to fate but you don't believe the billionaire thing? There's too much serendipity here."

Dmitry laughs and spits out some tuna by mistake. "Serendipity? I'm dead!"

Charlie smirks at Dmitry's eating habits. "You eat like an animal Dmitry."
"Sorry." Dmitry wipes his mouth.

CHAPTER SEVENTEEN

Dmitry's mom has a constant pained look on her face because she had a hip replacement done a couple of years ago. She has white hair which she dyes silver. Dmitry has her nose. It's quite large.

When he last saw her she scolded him about his sexuality and he became cross and left. Now she's here to visit him in the psych ward.

She swoops in like a fairy godmother and gives him a long wonderful hug.

"Thank Jesus that you are alright." She says and her voice is shaky.

Dmitry hadn't expected this pure of an emotion. He feels like a baby.

"It's ok sugar tot. I'm here." Mom soothes. "Who has been doing your laundry?"

Dmitry tells her that he has been doing it himself.

"When was the last time you did it?"

He tells her that it was a week ago.

"Do you have a washer and dryer here in the hospital?"
He nods.

"Wow, that's amazing."

They go to his room and mom looks around at the pencil drawings of the other patients. She scrutinizes the drawing of Charlie for an extra amount of time. "You have gotten really good at these."

He thanks her and sits down on his bed, his shoulders sagging. When mom's there, there's no reason to put up a fight against anything or anyone because mom is there and she is the strongest. That's clear. So he relaxes.

She starts collecting his dirty laundry. "Bring me to the laundry room."

He brings her to the laundry room and she starts a cycle.

"You look good sugar tot. You look manly. The beard suits you. I've always told you that being gay is not for you, you know."

He tells her again like he did as a little boy that it isn't a choice.

"You can say that all you want but you know the truth in your heart. Jesus didn't give you your parts and women their parts just so that you could pleasure yourselves separately. You're supposed to make babies. That's what we are here for. And not monkey babies like the evolutionists want us to believe. Human babies."

She seems determined and Dmitry can't do anything but nod. Besides, his love for her in this moment, as un-

expected as it was, makes him want to agree with her.
"Thank Jesus that you're alright. What about that man? That Bob?"

Dmitry tells her that he'll never see him again.

"Good. If you had told me about the way he was treating you I would have dealt with it."

He asks her how she would have dealt with it.

Mom smirks wickedly and winks. "I would have dealt with it, sugar tot."

Dmitry can't help but let out a small joyous giggle. Mom stares like a serial killer and nods. So he composes himself.

They talk for a while and when the laundry is done she irons and folds it.
"And what about the man that you beat up?"

Dmitry feels bad about that. The middle eastern guy didn't deserve to get stomped by his pink boots.

"Pink boots? Oh Dima Dima Dima." And it's clear what she means. The offense for which he is being punished by being in the psych ward isn't that he kicked a man repeatedly, it's that the boots were pink.

Dmitry agrees with her and tells her that he's been trying to be less provocative. And that he's developed an interest in a girl.

Mom gasps out of joy and hope that her son might be turning straight. “What’s her name?”

Dmitry tells her that her name is Charlie and he isn’t lying.

Mom can’t contain her excitement and hugs him a second time and then puts his neatly folded clothes BACK IN THE CLOSET.

Once she is done filling the closet with his things, she cups his face and kisses her good boy on both his cheeks and on his forehead. He finally sheds a tear out of love for her.

They hug for a third time. For a very long time and hold each other. Maybe she’s right. Maybe God does exist and maybe God did intend for Dmitry to be straight.

This kind of love… This kind of love… There’s no words really. It’s a wonder why Dmitry’s dad ran away.

CHAPTER EIGHTEEN

Charlie's dad is sitting in the garden on a bench beneath the tree with the white flowers. He's a round man with a happy red face. He's brought some cake in a pink box. Charlie has put on a flowery dress just for him and her hair has grown out a little.

When he sees Charlie coming down the cobblestone path towards him his face lights up even more and he stands up and holds out his arms.

They embrace for a long time and her dad starts crying. "I love you baby."

She tells him that she loves him too dad.

"How have they been treating you?"

She tells him that they have been treating her well.

"Have you been able to work from here?"

There's nothing much she can do. That client is gone.

He opens the box with the cake in it. He has brought two spoons and they both dig in. There is a couple of pieces of chocolate cake and a couple of pieces of strawberry cake, with very little icing because Charlie doesn't like it too sweet.

"I… I haven't seen you in a dress for such a long time." He confesses. "You look like your mother."

They both get distant in thought for a while. Charlie knows that she looks like her mother.

Charlie's mother passed away when Charlie was little. She only has a few memories of her face and her voice which she clings onto in times when she feels…

"It's like looking at her." Says dad.

Charlie doesn't like those words. She tries to change the subject and asks him what he thinks of the garden.

"It's well kept up. They must really put a lot of work into it. In my landscaping days I did this sort of work and I can tell you it's not easy to make something look so pretty." He stares at her again with that look in his eye. As if she were his mother.

Charlie never liked that look. It's too deep. But she understands it now. She musters up her courage and embraces her dad and kisses him on the cheek.

He snuffles. "You were such a cute little baby, baby. My baby. You were my baby. And your mother was so beautiful."

The word baby. It's a powerful word. Especially when combined with a loving embrace. It makes all kinds of things move inside a woman. Strange things. She suddenly remembers why she doesn't wear dresses.

Charlie pulls back abruptly.

"What's wrong?"

She tells him nothing. She was thinking of her friend

Dmitry. And it's true and it's ok. They keep eating cake and the amount of sugar is just right.

CHAPTER NINETEEN

There's a storm. With thunder and everything. The rain teems to earth at a 22.5 degree angle. The howling is so loud that Dmitry shuts the windows because he is afraid that they will rip out of their joints.

Lightning strikes the hillside so near. So near that the roar of the thunder makes his eardrums vibrate. The trees on the hillside sway like they are dancing. Perhaps it is God. God in the storm.

Dmitry's heart beats with a powerful rhythm and he can't sleep. He does pushups. 10 then 10 again then 10 then 10, until he feels the pain in his chest and his shoulders. Then he stands in front of the mirror in black boxer shorts. He's manly now. Perhaps like God intended.

It's what we believe isn't it? What makes our heart beat. What makes the pathways in our mind. Trauma stops some pathways but then new ones open up. With new pathways come new possibilities.

There's a knock and Dmitry goes to the door. It's Charlie, dressed in pajamas that have a flower pattern on them. She is shaking as if she were one of the trees in this storm.

"I can't sleep" She whispers.

He embraces her. "Neither can I."
"It's the storm."

"Yup."

"Do you want to sleep here?"
"Yes but no funny stuff."

They giggle.

"Ok I promise."

They lie down in Dmitry's bed together and hug as the earth twirls into chaos outside.

Charlie loves how Dmitry's shoulders feel or rather how they make her feel. We see ourselves in relation to others don't we? Dmitry makes her feel small and this again makes her feel protected.

Dmitry loves how small Charlie is and how when he embraces her, his arms reach all around her. This makes him feel big and as if he were protecting her. And in protecting her he feels protected by the world no matter how chaotic it is.

"We see ourselves in relation to other people don't we?" Charlie asks and Dmitry knows exactly what she means.

"Definitely."

He gives her a peck on the forehead. She looks up at him with those big fairytale eyes. She puckers her lips and they have an old fashioned kiss. Like one in the black and white movies. With the classical music and the wind blowing.

When they are done kissing they both breathe heavily. She can hear his big heart beat on his chest and he feels her little heart beat pounding on his belly.

"That was weird."

"I was about to say the same thing."

They giggle.

"Let's talk about something."

"Life in the nuthouse."

"There's quite a lot going on here isn't there?"

"Life without internet."

"It's a lot more enjoyable."

Charlie considers the thing she is about to say like a chess move. Then she asks. "What do you hope for in the future?"

Dmitry thinks for a moment and when the answer comes to him he has to hold back a minor tear. "To be honest. True love."

"Isn't that a cliché?"

"I don't care if it is. It's what I feel that I need."
Charlie is really nervous all of a sudden. "What I hope for is a cliché as well."

"What is it?"
"Someday in the future I want to be a mother. I want a child."

"That's not cliché. It's nature."

Charlie is genuinely relieved. She sighs.

"It's serendipity."

They giggle.

They fall asleep in one another's arms while the storm calms down and the trees begin to waltz more slowly and the rain becomes a drizzle and the lightning strikes so far away that the thunder is now just a growl.

CHAPTER TWENTY

A different evening. It's calm during a beautiful sunset which soaks the hills in purple. Charlie is lying awake in bed, thinking. Thinking about the kiss she shared with Dmitry. She is extremely turned on. She stops herself from gyrating her hips.

There's a knock. She freezes, then gets out of bed and goes to the door. It's Dmitry. He is bathed in purple light from her window. The look on his face. The look. She can only think of one thing. He wants to eat her.

They explode into each other's arms and kiss. The kiss is extremely sexual, with tongue and lip biting. He lifts her up and she wraps her legs around his waist. She feels his boner under her ass. A new feeling and it's so nice and she gyrates.

He carries her to bed and they make out and make out. He takes off her top and her nipples are a perfect pink and he goes insane. He sucks on them and won't stop.

"Oh baby." She says and pushes him back and takes off his top, revealing his broad shoulders.

They each admire the others body for a few moments. Their blood in their heads and their genitals. She sees the bulge in his boxers and pulls them down.

"It looks like an African elephant." She says.

"Thanks."

He leans back and she sucks. Her mouth is salivating and she can't stop. He feels the warmth and the wetness and groans.

Then he pushes her onto her back and pulls down her pajama bottoms. Her pussy. Her pussy. It's a perfect pink. His favorite color.

"It's pink." He breathes.

And the lips are little buns of bread. He goes down on her and runs his tongue along her slit. She feels the lovely invasion and her body jolts. Jolts.

They naturally turn like wheels into a 69 position and go at it for a long time. The last rays of purple sunlight shine in through the window and then it's dark.

He ejaculates into her mouth and she rationalizes about the taste and texture. It reminds her of some kind of food she has never tasted but liked.

She cums hard, gyrating her pink vagina against his mouth. His mouth opening and closing, eating and dabbing and devouring. The tickle she feels becomes a firework throughout her abdomen and into the rest of her body.

Afterwards they lie apart for a while. Ashamed and confused. Processing what had just happened.

"That was nice."

"It was."

"It was pretty great."

"Yeah… it was."

"It's natural."

"Maybe it is God. Like you said. Or some billionaires."

"Or just fate. Like you said."

"Maybe it's the head doctor who they won't let us meet."

"Yeah."

"Do you, do you mind if I sleep in my own bed. I have to process this."

"Me too. It's good."

Dmitry leans over and kisses her goodnight and they taste each other on their lips and he goes back to his room and they fall asleep separately.

CHAPTER TWENTY-ONE

The third night they had sex. It was awkward at first but then became amazing.

They had both been thinking about it since the last time. Thinking about it too much. Lain at night with their eyes open in their respective hospital rooms. Charlie was planning how it would go and Dmitry was in a marathon of being turned on and trying to think. Think anything coherently.

Charlie shows up at his room in a bathrobe under which she is hiding pink lingerie which she had bought at a sex shop down the street from the hospital. Pink is Dmitry's favorite color and she imagined it made her look like one of those fairytale creatures he always dreamed about.

Dmitry hadn't showered that day and had no idea whatsoever that she would show up when she did. He is wearing the same black boxer shorts he had been wearing since the 69, unwashed. His beard is untrimmed and his teeth are stained from coffee he had had that day.

But to her he just smells musky and looks rugged. A real man. Some kind of animal.

And to him, she indeed does look like a fairy princess when she opens her robe and lets it drop to the floor. A fairytale princess outside of himself. Right there.

"Are we doing this?" He asks.

She nods. "Yes."

They begin by touching each other's bodies. Both of their breathing quickens and he draws her closer to him, pressing his penis against her belly.

They kiss and she tastes the coffee. He undoes her bra and sucks on her nipples. She drops to her knees and pulls down his dirty boxers and places his penis in her mouth, never breaking eye contact with him. It's a bit awkward for him.

But it's ok. She runs the head of his elephant trunk across her thick lips and then flicks her tongue against his tip. Then she sucks again.

He is driven by a powerful urge and pulls her up by her armpits and places her on his shoulders. She moves her pink underwear to the side and he starts eating her out. She ducks so as not to hit her head on the ceiling. It's a bit awkward for her.

But it's ok. He drops her onto the bed and gets on top of her. They make eye contact.

"Ok?"

"Ok."

She is entered by him. He enters her.

She has felt vibrators and dildos that promised to have a realistic fleshy feel to them but what she has inside of her now feels different. It is warm and spongy and hard in the right place.

He has fucked men in the ass before but this definitely is different. It is much more accommodating and naturally lubricated. Its cleaner and it smells nice and the shape and muscles inside pull at his penis.

The rest of what they did was hump. That's the best way to describe it. There were too many new sensations and emotions. The looks on both their faces were the same. It was wonder. It sounds cliché but it was wonder.

Their mouths wide open. And their eyes too. Their eyebrows furrowed and unfurrowed. The occasional squeak from her and grunt from him. A look at the ceiling. At the bed board. And then the eyes again.

Hump hump. Huump. Hump.

Different rhythms. Whatever felt right.

Her hands on his ass, guiding him sometimes. His arms hooked underneath hers.

A kiss. A peck. A REAL KISS. A peck. A kiss.

Her heart exploding and his too. Blood to the head and to the groin.

Hump hump hump hump hump hump and FIRE FUCKING WORKS.

They cum at the same time. The sensations different. His shorter and more focused on the groin. Hers throughout her body.

He cums inside her. A fountain of jizz filling her gourd.

Cliché beautiful. Nothing more but nothing fucking less either.

Afterwards they lie together, hugging and panting and kissing each other. Charlie has never had sex with a man before and so she doesn't know much about protection.

Dmitry hasn't had sex with a woman and so he doesn't know either and so he didn't use any. So there's a chance of pregnancy.

And that's how some little things start.

CHAPTER TWENTY-TWO

A few weeks later and Dmitry is drawing Charlie in the nude as she lies on her back on his bed.

He's drawing with pencil and taking in the details. The wavelike curves that when put together create her whole body.

When he gets to her belly he makes a stroke that is rounder than usual and this startles him. Why is her belly so round? He looks up at Charlie in real life.

The bed is like a lake and Charlie is a swan. The blanket is wrinkled like waves on water. Charlie's belly is plump.

"Did you put on weight?" He sounds like a doofus.
Charlie feels his eyes and looks at him, concerned. "I missed my period."

"What do you mean?"

"I'm pregnant."

Charlie looks at his drawing again. Yes, the belly is bigger and yes it is bigger in real life as well.

He puts away the piece of paper and pencil. He gets up and walks over to her and stands awkwardly for a few moments beside her. She takes his hand and places it on her belly.

He feels heat.

"There's no movement."

"It's too early for that."

Dmitry's eyes start to water and his knees slowly bend. He puts his ear to her belly.

"It's too early to hear too."

"I know."

She rubs his head and his knees connect with the floor.

Dmitry feels like he's in a cave. But instead of walls, the cave is made up of a circle of light.

Charlie feels like a freshly picked pear. Yummy and fleshy and small.

Dmitry raises his head. "What are we going to do?"

Charlie's lower lip starts to quiver. "Well we can't tell anyone."

"Why not?"

"It's part of the rules they set for me. No sexual contact."

"So what?"

"I could go to jail."

Dmitry looks like a doofus. “Yes. Right.”
“I can’t get an abortion either because I can’t leave.”

Dmitry remembers what his mother said. “We’re supposed to make babies. That’s what we are here for.”

“What do you mean?”

“It’s what God wants. Our parts. They’re made for this. I mean… I wouldn’t want you to get an abortion.”

Charlie’s lower lip starts to outright quake. “You can keep God out of it. I want to keep the baby anyways.”

“We’ll figure out a way”

“If I go to jail, then so be it.” Tears pour from her eyes but her face is motionless.

“We’ll hide it. You have to eat a lot to put on weight.”

“Ok.”

“There’s only two months left to go and then you’re free. We can hide it that long.”

“Ok…”

CHAPTER TWENTY-THREE

They're sitting in group therapy, a couple of seats apart. Charlie feels like a little boat. She's wearing loose fitting clothing but is so aware of her condition that she is getting paranoid.

Dr. Me keeps looking over at her while the other patients speak about their previous night and the upcoming day.

Dmitry also notices Dr. Me's strange interest in Charlie and he too becomes worried.

The woman who looks like a 1950s patient who has the scar on her head as if she had been lobotomized is crying. "I hurt my friend yesterday."

"No you didn't" says the sleepwalker with the paper crown. "I'm fine."

"No, I hurt you."

"You must have been dreaming. You didn't hurt me."

Dr. Me smiles warmly "You didn't hurt anybody. Ok next."

It's the old couple's turn. The husband came to the ward early again to support his wife. "We are thinking about getting a pistol."

Dr. Me turns towards them "I don't think that's a good idea."

"Well we no longer feel safe."

"I definitely don't think that getting a gun will make anyone safer."

"Well, we want one."

"For here?" Asks Dr. Me.

"No. For our home."

Dr. Me frowns. "Ok."

The lady with the scar on her head interrupts. "I also want a gun."

"Nobody is getting a gun ok?" Dr. Me makes eye contact with all the patients at once. "Ok, next."

It's Charlie's turn and she is nervous. "I slept well. And today I'm not going to do much."

Dr. Me looks at her belly again and then up at her face. She adjusts her clothing uncomfortably.

Dmitry steps in. "And me too, I'm not going to do much. I might take a walk in the garden but that's all.

Dr. Me turns to him. "Wait your turn please." He returns his attention towards Charlie. "Are you ok?"

Charlie nods. "Yes of course. Why wouldn't I be?"

Dr. Me SNIFFS.

Neither Charlie nor Dmitry react. Dr. Me glares apprehensively.

CHAPTER TWENTY-FOUR

At lunch Charlie and Dmitry are sitting together at a small table away from the other patients and out of sight of the nurses and doctors. Charlie has a burger and Dmitry some kind of soup-like slosh.

Charlie is visibly shaken. "What do I do?"

"Eat." Says Dmitry.

Charlie bites off a mouthful of burger and then starts to chew laboriously. Dmitry nods and looks around. No one is watching or listening.

Charlie swallows. "I'm not that hungry."

"But that's the plan."

"Did you see Dr. Me? How he looked at me? He knows."

"Not necessarily. It may just have been a coincidence."

"Yes, you're right." Her lip starts to quiver and then she takes another bite of her burger.

"What is it now?"

She chews for a long time and then swallows and then speaks. "What do I tell my friends? Am I still gay?"

Dmitry is perplexed. "We tell our friends the truth. That we're bisexual."

"Who will take care of the baby? Will it be you or me?"

"Sh. Don't say that word too loud."

"B… baby?"

"Yeah."

"Ok. But who will take care of it?"

"Well we will. Together." Dmitry says matter of factly.

She smiles, her eyes glisten and she nods. "Yeah ok."

She takes another bite and chews and then swallows. "Am I bisexual?"

Dmitry contemplates the question. "Well I'm not sure about you. But I… I don't feel bisexual. I don't feel straight either. I feel. Love. I feel Charlie sexual."

"Charlie sexual?" She beams and shines.

"Yeah. It's like the label doesn't matter. It's just you that matters. And its gotten stronger ever since."

"Ever since I got… the P word?

"Yeah."

"It's the same for me. I'm Dmitry sexual."

Dmitry looks at her lovingly and she looks back at him and it feels like there's a giant glittering heart of energy around them which keeps them safe and it feels like the mermaids and the tropical birds, the fairies and the antelope are all breathing from within Charlie and Dmitry's lungs. Lending them their hearts to make their hearts beat thrice as strong. And there is beauty in this heart of energy. Pure. Beauty. Like in a movie or a book.

SQUEAK!

A speaker comes on and an excited voice yells in a high frequency. "This is Dr. Me addressing the head doctor, Dr. Eternal. We have a situation in the dining hall! A situation in the dining hall! Two patients are planning something! It's the Fairy and the Elephant! Please report to the dining hall and pick them up for the next part of therapy! They are ready! I repeat! They are ready!"

SQUEAK!

Ready? The fairy and the elephant? The head doctor is coming to pick them up? Charlie and Dmitry are perplexed. They look around…

The other patients are staring at them blank faced like robots. No emotion. No life in their eyes. Just cold stares. The lobotomized lady. The old couple. The sleepwalker with the paper crown on his head and all the other patients.

A man that looks like a frog flicks out his tongue and licks a spoon. Then he too becomes blank faced and glowers at them.

"Wh... what the fuck is going on?" Charlie feels a shiver go down her spine and a fear for her baby.

Dmitry squares his shoulders and sticks out his chin and balls his fists. "Hey. People. What's happening?"

They other patients answer by shaking their heads in unison, like robots.

Suddenly there's footsteps coming closer from down the hallway. Someone is walking very quickly towards the dining room. Step step step step.

Charlie gets hysterical. "Why won't you speak? Who is coming down the hallway?"

The other patients stop shaking their heads and gawk at her belly.

"Stop! Stop them from staring, Dmitry! Stop them!"

The footsteps get louder as they come closer. Clack clack clack. Whoever is coming is large.

Dmitry jumps up and squares himself up against the others. "What's going on! Tell us! Tell us who's coming!" He balls his fists like he's about to fight.

Charlie hides under the table.

The footsteps stop by the doorway and then…

…the Eternal Boxer rounds the corner, wearing a doctor's coat. He has five large bumps on his head from fights he was in. Some he won and some he lost. Each of the bumps has a face and a personality. The bumps have eyes and noses and mouths. One leers and another frowns and another laughs. One bump's mouth is another bumps eye.

He has boxing gloves for hands. Boxing gloves eternally glued to his wrists. Although he no longer boxes for a living. He is now the head doctor of a psych ward. A very good one at that. In this psych ward he brings people together. He creates families.

"Allow me to introduce myself. I'm Dr. Eternal, I'm the head doctor here. Please come with me, I have something for the two of you." He holds out his gloved right hand.

Dmitry flinches and lifts up his fists. The bumps on the Eternal Boxer's head start laughing.

"Oh please." The Eternal Boxer says. "I no longer fight.

Just shake my hand already."

Dmitry hesitantly lowers his fists and then shakes the Eternal Boxer's glove. "Hi. I'm Dmitry and this is… Charlie."

Charlie emerges from her hiding spot. The Eternal Boxer smiles at her and there is love in his left eye and madness in his right eye. The bumps on his head also smile, some of them are even smitten.

She also shakes his glove.

"Follow me." The Eternal Boxer leads Charlie and Dmitry past the other patients who are still in a trance-like state.

He leads the lovers out of the silent dining hall. Down the long ominous hallway. Up some infinite stairs. And into his odd office.

CHAPTER TWENTY-FIVE

Dear Reader,

As you know of my past as a boxer, I bet that you are surprised to find that my present position is that of head doctor at a psychiatric facility. The truth is that I, upon reflection, surprise myself as well.

What happened was that once I won my last fight against Alex and Claire and attained the most highly coveted prize in the universe, the prize of the family, the father the mother and the child, I began reflecting on my life.

I had never known my mother and father. Rather was I an orphan left and found on the doorstep of a boxing gym. The owner of the boxing gym, a man they called the G.O.A.T, saw my potential and decided to take me in. He raised me, but he also used me as an animal to experiment on. He wanted to create the most supreme fighter that he could. Body and mind. And so what he did was devise a training plan which involved some questionable tactics.

The physical training regimen was brutal. He would wake me up at 3 am at which time I would then go jogging for two hours. At 5 am I would do weight training for another two hours, after which I would have my breakfast and an hour long break. From 8am until 1pm I would train combinations and footwork after which I would have another hour long break and lunch. From 2pm until 7pm I would then spar against multiple opponents, one after another, quite a few of them much larger and better at boxing than I was and I would get hurt. Then I would finally have free time until exactly 10pm, which was bedtime.

The mental training was even more cruel and what made it so effective was that I was not aware of it happening. He used the fact that I didn't have a family to motivate me. He would allow me to have dinner with him and his family once in a while but he would not allow me to feel as if I was part of it. In this way he guided me towards wanting nothing more than a family of my own. Or in this case, the most coveted prize in the universe.

But the mental training didn't stop there. He would also literally guide my thoughts through a kind of shock therapy. You see he was very rich from all the fights that he had won throughout his career and he was able to create an army of humanoid snake robots that would follow me and annoy me everywhere I went. If they saw that my mind was drifting away from the fight, they would SNIFF really loudly.

Now you might be asking, why would the Eternal Boxer compare a SNIFF to an electric shock? Well the answer is: one SNIFF is alright but a million SNIFFS throughout your life… that's horror. Especially if they only come when you begin to dream your own thoughts. These SNIFFS were like hornet stings, keeping me on track as a boxer and limiting my free will. That which makes us human.

Once I had won the family I decided to hang my boxing career to the wall and become a psychiatrist so that I could fully understand the damage that had been done to me. But first I murdered the G.O.A.T by beating his old ass into pulp. Even his bones gave way and crumbled as they crunched under my angry fists. I do feel sorry now that I did that. I loved the old man and I realize that I am who I am today because of him. But there's no reason to keep dwelling on the past.

I inherited all of what was the G.O.A.T's. The money, the gym, the humanoid snake robots. And now wait until you hear what I did with all of this fortune.

Eternally yours,
Dr. Eternal

CHAPTER TWENTY-SIX

There is a beautiful couple sitting across my desk at the psych ward. The girl Charlie is of Anglo-Saxon descent with a hint of Middle-Eastern to her and the boy Dmitry is as ginger as a Ukrainian can get.

They were both homosexual a few months ago when I first read about them in a book while travelling by spaceship to my last professional boxing match. Now they are lovesexual and not only that, the girl is pregnant. My treatment plan worked.

They think that they're in trouble. I solemnly ask who the father is.

"It's me." Says the boy.

I nod gravely.

"What's going to happen to us?" The girl asks.

Suddenly I grin. "You are going to get married."

The two look at each other with bewilderment.

"Married?"

"Yes" I say.

"What do you mean? Aren't we in trouble for breaking the rules of the psych ward?" Dmitry is perplexed.

I laugh heartily and so do the bumps on my head. "No. You're not in trouble. I guarantee it."

"What are those things?" Dmitry points at my bumps.

"They're my friends. They help me remember things. Specifically they help me remember every time I got hit in the head and why."

Dmitry is annoyed. "Ok, I can accept the faces on your head but what kind of hospital is this?"

I smile at the couple. "This hospital is a secret testing

facility which belongs to me. I use it to try to undo a wrong which was done to me all my life. You see I was never allowed to have a family. So here, I created a family using the two of you."

"So you created our relationship?" Charlie is flustered.

"Yes." I respond.

"I… I knew it…" She stutters.

Dmitry cuts in "Are you from earth?"

"Yes… but us billionaires get to travel all around the universe. So I've travelled in ways you don't even know about and been to planets you can't even dream about. And been witness to scientific discoveries that they don't tell you about because you would never be able to afford them."

"I told you it was a billionaire." Charlie whispers to Dmitry who looks perplexed.

"So… you've been watching us all this time?" Dmitry's voice is soft.

"More like stalked you. But don't ask how I've stalked you. You wouldn't understand."

Charlie leans forward and reveals her cleavage. A gesture meant to manipulate me for information. "Why was everyone staring at us? Is this place real?" She asks.

I decide to be completely honest with her. "Yes it is real. And it is on earth. But it is filled with humanoid snake robots and the three of us are the only actual living beings in the building.

I have been guiding the two of you on a journey to exactly where you are now by using SNIFFS. You both started out as one hundred percent homosexual but now you are lovesexual and we have a pregnancy to prove it."

Charlie is skeptical. “Lovesexual?”

“It’s a new kind of sexuality that I discovered.”

“That’s not how these things work.” Says Dmitry. “You can’t just create a sexuality. And you can’t change anyone’s sexuality either.”

I chuckle. “I didn’t create or change anything. I just awoke what was naturally within you. You see, homosexuality, heterosexuality, and all other forms of sexuality… they are all the same thing. All part of the same interconnected star. Love.”

“What is this all about?”

I exhale “It’s all about you and me.”

“What do you mean?”

“Well you are my family.” I am at the same time embarrassed and can barely hold back my excitement. “The three of you.”

“That’s creepy.” Dmitry shakes his head. “And why do you have boxing gloves for hands?”

“My foster father glued them onto my wrists when I was a child.”

Dmitry is taken aback and he begins to COUGH. His reaction makes me feel REJECTED AND IT HURTS MY FEELINGS!

“So you want us to get married?” Inquires Charlie.

“Yes. I have it all planned out. The craziest wedding in history. With all your friends present.”

“But you made us fall in love so how do we know that our love is real?”

“Oh it’s real. I just helped you think in a certain direction and helped you meet. You see… the man who raised me used the same SNIFFS and humanoid snake robots my whole life to make sure that I would never know affection. It was torture. But when he died I decided to use these same techniques for the opposite. For family. Famiglia. Familie. Famila. Rodzina. Gimene. Oikogeneia."

"You know how crazy you sound right?" Dmitry is red in the face from coughing so much.

"Yes. I do. And it gets crazier. I will now give you a choice."

"A choice?"

"A choice. Are you ready?"

The boy and the girl look each other in the eyes.

"All I know is that I love you." Charlie says.

"I love you too." Dmitry replies.

"OK we're ready. What's the choice?"

I nod and smile. "You have a choice between the two following ways to proceed in this story:"

"If you want Charlie and Dmitry to fight against the humanoid snake robots then continue reading chapter 27."

"If you want Dmitry and Charlie to get married now then skip to chapter 28."

CHAPTER TWENTY-SEVEN

Dmitry and Charlie rush down the infinite stairway. It seems to go on forever. Was it this long before? They rush down even faster, determined to leave the psych ward come what may. Let the cops get them. They don't care.

They almost stumble over the old man and woman from their ward. The couple is blocking their path.

Dmitry grabs the old man by his shoulders and urges him to "Get out of here. The head doctor is a psychopath!"

But the old people don't respond. Creepy creepy. Instead they just stand still, blocking the way down the stairs.

Charlie shouts at the old woman. "Let us through!"

SKREE!

The old people screech! They suddenly grow serpent's tails and their heads split open vertically, revealing robotic rows of razor sharp iron teeth.

"Humanoid snake robots!" Charlie yells!

The humanoid snake robots screech a robotic screech as if to call for backup.

SKREE! SKREE!

"Oh shit." Charlie exclaims. "Do something."

Dmitry kicks the old man in the chest with his pink boots, hard and the old man goes flying down the stairs.

He hits a wall and breaks apart like a metal windup toy. Screws and wheels go flying all over the place. His serpent's tail rips off and flip flops around in a pool of blood.

SKREEE!

It's the old woman and she's going for Charlie. Charlie holds her back but her vertical robot jaws are getting closer and closer to Charlie's face.

Dmitry grabs the old woman from behind and throws her over the railing. She plummets multiple storeys and then shatters when she hits the bottom floor.

"Ok let's go!" Dmitry takes Charlie's hand and they continue down the stairs. They reach the ominous hallway and immediately have to slow down again. They see a creepy silhouette. It's the 1950's patient. The patient sees them and her head cracks open at the scar to reveal that she too is a humanoid robot lizard.

"Oh shit" Charlie looks around for a weapon. She finds a Persian sabre hanging conveniently from the wall which she grabs with both hands.

"Ahh!" Charlie yells and runs at the creature, her pregnant belly swaying back and forth.

SKREE!

The humanoid robot lizard lunges and Charlie swipes down, slicing the thing in two. Blood from the humanoid parts squirts against the walls and a few metal parts clank onto the floor.

"Good job." Says Dmitry.

He takes her hand again and they run down the hallway past the dining hall. Suddenly a swarm of humanoid snake robots erupts from the dining room doorway and rushes after them. Leading the swarm is the sleepwalker with the paper crown and bumbling along last is the one that looks like a frog.

SKREE! SKREE! SKREE!

Charlie runs as fast as she can with her pregnant belly and the Persian sabre she is holding. Dmitry lets her overtake him so that he can make up the rear and protect her in case one of the humanoid snake robots catches up to them.

They round the corner to the entrance to the ward and come to an abrupt stop. Dr. Me is guarding the entrance to the ward. He is also a humanoid snake robot. He opens his mouth vertically and screeches.

SKREE!

They are now caught between two fronts. Dr. Me ahead of them and a whole horde of humanoid snake robots behind them approaching fast.

So, Charlie and Dmitry take the opportunity to kiss passionately in the face of such horror and danger.

And then it's on.

Charlie twirls like a deadly ballerina, slicing humanoid snake robots apart left and right and Dmitry stomps and kicks the shit out of the humanoid snake robots with his pink boots.

Dmitry crushes the paper-crowned head of the sleepwalker against the floor and Charlie slices off Dr. Me's tail and then feeds it to him. They slice and stomp and slice and stomp until they are standing in a giant puddle of electric toaster parts and gore.

They kiss passionately again.

Charlie finds a keycard in Dr. Me's pocket and they jog over to the gate.

But the keycard doesn't work. She tries again and again. It doesn't work.

"Here let me try." Says Dmitry. But it still doesn't work.

SQUEAK!

The hospital speaker has come on again.

"Nope nope nope." They hear the Eternal Boxers voice. "This was a test too. To see how you would work together and if you truly passionately love one another."

Dmitry and Charlie look at each other in confusion.

The Eternal Boxer continues. "And you passed. Obviously."

Charlie shouts "What do you want!? What do you want from us!?"

"What I want?" The voice echoes through the gore stained corridors. "I want you two to get married. I mean. Don't you want to get married?"

They look each other in the eye and consider the question. Everything they had been through. Everything leading to this point. Charlie had been right. It was orchestrated. And it does feel beautiful.

Charlie smiles and grabs Dmitry's strong arms. "Yes, we want to get married. Don't we? I mean don't you?"

Dmitry giggles and his giggles echo throughout the facility and he drops to one knee. "I'm the man. I'm the one who should be proposing, not you, so. Charlie. Will you be my wife?"

"Yes. Eternally." She drops down to her knees too and kisses Dmitry.

The Eternal Boxer pokes his head around the corner, grinning. He laughs heartily and so do the bumps on his head.

HAHAHA!

"Oh how beautiful!" He bellows.

CHAPTER TWENTY-EIGHT

BANG!

There is a flash of light and Dmitry finds himself standing by an altar in the middle of an African savannah. It's the day of the wedding. There are guests seated underneath a clean white cloth which occasionally whips in the wind.

Claire de Lune by Debussy is playing from an old gramophone. It resonates across the grasslands. There are giraffes in the distance and specks of green where there are trees.

Dmitry looks down at himself. He is wearing a suit and his hands are larger than normal and gray and he has a trunk like an elephant instead of a nose. He is alarmed.

Next to Dmitry stands the Eternal Boxer. He is wearing a preacher's collar and holding a bible and grinning and all the bumps on his head have thoughtful expressions on their faces. "Don't worry Dmitry. You're an elephant now."

Dmitry looks out at the guests. It seems that everyone from his side is there. His mom, crossing herself at the sight of the Eternal Boxer. Snort the black bartender, looking for a way out. Gay Mohammed, feeling uncomfortable at a Christian wedding. The old homeless guy that told Dmitry to "just live" that one night in the park. Even Bob, that fucking asshole. He came to the wedding.

Dmitry doesn't recognize many of the faces on Charlie's side. He once read somewhere that it's important to have separate friends to make a relationship last, so he isn't too worried.

But then he thinks where is Charlie?

In that moment the bridal chorus from Wagner's Lohengrin begins to play.

Charlie is standing under a baobab tree for some shade. Baobab trees are the fattest trees on earth so there is a lot of shade. She is standing there with her father who looks extremely anxious. Her belly has gotten bigger and she is close to giving birth. She is holding a bouquet of flowers and wearing a simple white wedding gown and dad is wearing a tuxedo.

Charlie seems to have grown butterfly wings with circles of different colors on them. She is perplexed as to where the wings came from. She is able to move them by moving the muscles in her back, so yes, they are real.

She flaps them slowly at first and then speeds up. Her feet leave the ground and she hovers over her father laughing joyously, as does he.

"Where did you get those wings from baby?"

"I don't know. They just appeared dad."

In that moment the bridal chorus from Wagner's Lohengrin begins to echo across the savannah.

Charlie drops back down to earth and looks around for the source of the noise. She spots a white tent in the distance. More of a cloth whipping in the wind but there are people under it.

"Shall we go baby?"

"Yes daddy."

She hugs her father tightly and flaps her wings. The two of them lift up into the air and fly towards the tent. Underneath them herds of buffalo and antelope drink from rivers and run through green grass.

They land by the entrance to the tent. Dad kisses her on the cheek and then leads her down the aisle to the altar over a long Persian carpet.

She looks around and sees that everyone is there. Tammy and You, dressed in pink and bawling their eyes out when they realize that Charlie is pregnant. The man she hit in the face with a brick and his wife and son, who is now 3 years old and a bit taller. The toddler keeps squiggling around and can't sit still. The old couple from the hospital, still holding hands after all those years together. The woman with the scar on her head. The frog man and the sleepwalker with the paper crown.

There are also some faces she doesn't recognize. There's a two headed giant, one side male and one side female and a whole row of men in boxing robes. The Eternal Boxer is standing by the altar dressed as an officiant and next to him…

It's Dmitry but he looks different. Charlie can barely hold back her excitement. Dmitry has somehow morphed into an elephant. His nose is long and soft, his ears large wide fans. His skin is gray.

Dad leads Charlie down the aisle towards Dmitry as the bridal chorus from Wagner's Lohengrin plays and she walks to the rhythm and it's beautiful.

I am tremendously enthusiastic. All my work and all that I've ever desired is about to culminate. The heads on my head keep me calm but inside I'm bursting like little bombs going off in my unconscious mind.

I look at Dmitry. How handsome he is as an elephant. His nose so long and powerful. Straight out of Charlie's imagination. He's hyper ventilating as Charlie walks down the aisle and his trunk toots a little.

And I look at Charlie the fairy. I gave her butterfly wings with multi colored circles on them. Now she really is a fairy-tale creature. Straight out of Dmitry's imagination. Her gait is mighty and her belly round.

Charlie and dad reach the altar and dad begins to cry when he gives her away to Dmitry.

Dad takes a seat.

The two lovers lock hands and lock eyes. Charlie's inner strength visibly calms Dmitry. And Dmitry's playful character gives Charlie strength.

Now it is my turn to speak.

"Dearly beloved. We are gathered here today to witness and celebrate the union of Charlie and Dmitry in marriage. Once on different sides of a river, they are now proof that the only thing that truly matters in the matters of love is love. Today is proof that this river can be swum across and as we create this marriage we also create a new bond and a new sense of family – one that will undoubtedly include all that are present here today."

You and Tammy gasp for air, they are crying so much. On the other side of the aisle Snort the gay bartender and Gay Mohammed fall into each other's arms and also start crying.

"Now please if you would exchange your vows." I say. "Dmitry, you may start."

Dmitry rummages around in his pockets, looking for the piece of paper that he had written his vows on. He uses his elephant trunk like a third arm to save time. He finds the vows and holds them up in front of his face with his trunk.

"I vow to always treat you like the princess you are. I vow to covet you whenever you want me to and to be overprotective of you whenever you want me to. But when you don't want my attention, I vow to stay out of your way. I vow to cook for you when you are tired and to share the household chores with you. I vow to raise our child in a mutually agreed way with the goal, of making them extremely intelligent and physically healthy. To achieve this goal I vow to use reward and punishment. I vow to stay with you and our child until the day I die no matter how hard times may get. I vow to argue with you about anything that you may want to argue about no matter how trivial it seems to me. I vow to not give up."

Dmitry the elephant looks up from the paper and at Charlie who's eyes are now watering.

Dmitry puts away his list of vows and Charlie withdraws hers from between her boobs. Although she is composed her wings flutter and unconsciously give away her exhilaration.

She starts reading. "I vow to always treat you like the beast that you are. I vow to make you feel strong and masculine. But I also vow to allow you to be weak within my arms when you need to be. I vow to cook and clean most of the time. I vow to raise our child to be highly intelligent and physically strong. I vow to use psychological training techniques which come naturally to me as a mother in order to achieve this goal. I vow to never go behind your back with anyone about anything and I vow to argue with you through everything until we have found a solution, no matter how trivial it seems to me."

There is no dry eye in the place. Even I, the Eternal Boxer, shed a tear and so do the bumps on my head.

The frog man ribbits.

I croak "And now please exchange rings."

Charlie withdraws a ring from her cleavage and Dmitry withdraws a ring from his suit-pocket with his trunk. The rings are pure gold and have hearts engraved on them.

Dmitry's elephant ears stick out and his head looks like a heart. Charlie's butterfly wings stick out and her body looks like a heart.

Dmitry takes Charlie's hand with his hands and places the ring on her finger.

"With this ring I thee wed."

Charlie takes Dmitry's hand and places the ring on her finger.

"With this ring I thee wed."

I'm finally totally crying and the explosions in my body have moved to the bumps on my head and they are crying too. I haven't had a good cry in ages and so I just let it all out."I now pronounce thee… I now… I… I'm sorry I'm crying."

The situation has humor to it because the officiant isn't supposed to cry. A few of the guests laugh through their own tears, lovingly and with understanding. So do Dmitry and Charlie.

"You're not supposed to be crying." Charlie blubbers.

Dmitry lets out a chortle.

Soon everyone is laughing uncontrollably. What a beautiful wedding.

I compose myself as much as I can. "I now... pronounce thee... husband and wife. You may kiss the bride!

The guests all cheer.

Dmitry and Charlie connect hands and slowly move closer to one another. Kissing is a bit of a funny challenge as they have never kissed with Dmitry's trunk in the way before.

They giggle and make it work.

They kiss.

Dmitry's ears flutter and so do Charlie's wings. They both lift off the ground and it is a truly unique kiss. Uniqueness.

Bob takes pictures with an expensive professional camera.

What a wedding. What a ceremony. My bumps and I beam up at the hovering couple.

Their heads touch the white cloth and they suddenly realize that they are both flying. They laugh whole-heartedly and kiss again and then twirl in the air.

The cheering intensifies.

CHAPTER TWENTY-NINE

The twirling continues at the party. As all the other guests dance on the ground, Dmitry and Charlie dance in the air while the sun goes down on the purple African hills.

I put on a skimpy red dress and pull a blonde wig over my bumps and then I take over the DJ booth. I spin a list of classics from throughout the ages. My Way by Sinatra, The Mighty Quinn by Dylan, Black Cat Hoot Owl Blues by Ma Rainey.

Black cat on my doorstep, black cat on my windowsill
Black cat on my doorstep, black cat on my windowsill
If one black cat don't cross me, another black cat will

It's bad luck if I'm jolly, bad luck if I cry
It's bad luck if I'm jolly, bad luck if I cry
It's bad luck if I stay here, it's still more bad luck if I die
It's all outside now.

Snort and Mohammed are slow dancing. Tammy and You are grinding on each other. The old homeless man and Bob are making out behind the stage. The man who's face Charlie broke is dancing in a cute circle with his wife and his son who is bunny hopping to the rhythms. The old couple is breakdancing as they are humanoid robot lizards anyways and not really old. The 1950s mental patient with the scar on her head is dancing the tango with Dr. Me even though the beat is wrong. The frog man and the sleepwalker with the paper crown are drinking heavily at the bar.

Dmitry's mom is sitting alone at a table, drinking lots of sparkling water when Charlie's dad approaches her.

"Hi, I don't think we've formally met. I'm the father of the bride."

"And I'm the mother of the groom."

"May I take a seat?"

She sizes him up for a moment. "Fine."

Dad sits down and looks at her glass. "Don't you drink alcohol?"

"No. Never have in Jesus's name."

Dad nods. "That's a good credo." He pours himself a glass of water.

"So what do you think of this… devilishness?" She asks.

He reflects on her question. "I'm not really religious, but I have noticed that it's a bit of a strange wedding."

"What did you notice?"

"Well for one, my daughter has butterfly wings."

Mom nods. "And my son is an elephant. So if it's not devilishness, what would you call it?"

"Maybe science? The last thing I remember my child was in the psych ward for beating that man over there with a brick." He points at the man and his family.

"With a brick? It's quite similar to what I remember."

"What's that?

"My son was in the psych ward for stomping that Muslim man over there with his pink boots. But that's not the craziest thing about this wedding."

"What is?

"My son used to be gay. Not bisexual, not just a little gay, all out shaking his ass when he walked and dyeing his hair gay."

Dad's eyes widen. "Now I remember… my daughter used to be gay as well."

Mom nods. "Devilishness."

Dad shakes his head. "Science."

Mom frowns. "Maybe it's the same thing."

Dad smiles. "Would you like to dance?"

Mom's frown turns into an expression of interest for a moment. But then she frowns again. "I don't dance."

In that moment one of the bumps on my head whispers to me to put on bluegrass gospel music and I do.

Oh happy day (oh happy day)
Oh happy day (oh happy day)
When Jesus washed (when Jesus washed)
He washed my sins away (oh happy day)

He taught me how to watch, fight and pray, fight and pray
And live rejoicing every day

Mom suddenly starts shaking uncontrollably.

"Are you ok? Do you need some water?" Dad asks.

"Dear Jeeesus!" Yells mom and kicks away her chair and starts dancing.

She grabs dad's hands and pulls him to the dance floor and they go at it. The other guests all erupt in applause.

The party goes on until late at night. When I notice that the guests are getting sleepy Ma Rainey suddenly shows up in person and starts performing Jelly Bean. One of the bumps on my head yawns the others are excited to see her in the flesh and poke out from under my wig.

Ma Rainey sings.
My daddy left me this morning
That's why I moan and cry
He'll make you laugh he'll make you cry
He'll drive those blues away
You'll sit right down and weep and moan
And then you'll find he's went
Lord, I been wonderin' where my jelly bean has gone

It's now time for the father and daughter dance. Dad and Charlie hug each other and Charlie rotates them up into the cool night air.

Lions roar and hyenas laugh and crickets chirp. The night sky is bright with stars and a moon that you can only see in Africa.

Mom dances with Dmitry. They hug tightly and Dmitry flaps his ears and lifts her up into the sky as well.

The other guests have stopped dancing and are now sitting at the tables eating leftovers and drinking sparkling water.

The wedding was a success. A real real success.

Suddenly Charlie's belly begins to STING.

She feels something break. It's what you call her water breaking. The water rains down onto the dance floor.

"Oh shit." She says.
"What is it?" Dad asks.

"The baby is coming."
Charlie has less than a second to decide. Drop dad and catch the baby coming out of her or hold onto dad and let the baby fall to the ground. It's between dad and the baby.

She makes the decision that I secretly hoped she would make. She decides against the child.

The baby slides out of her vagina and falls for 29 meters while SCREAMING A PRIMAL SCREAM. Dad looks horrified as his daughter clings to him.

Dmitry drops his mom and tries to catch the baby but he isn't fast enough.

The baby hits the ground with it's head first and a bump appears that has eyes and a nose and a mouth. The baby is knocked out cold and the bump takes over the earsplitting SHRIEKING.

Mom also hits the ground and her legs immediately SNAP SNAP.

The guests gasp.

Before anyone knows what's going on, I push Ma Rainey out of the way violently and jump off the stage. I run to the baby and snatch it up and keep running in the direction of the hills.
I am stealing the baby.
My red dress rides up as I run.
My blonde wig falls off.

CHAPTER THIRTY

“My baby!” Charlie screams and lowers herself and her dad back down onto the ground. She lets her dad go and looks around for the child.

Dmitry yells. “Where is the baby!?”

His mom is lying on the floor with her legs snapped forward at the knees. She is moaning, her mind is not quite there anymore. Dad goes and tends to her.

The guests run around headless, some soothe each other, others hide. Everything is chaos.

Ma Rainey stands up and dusts herself off and yells “The drag queen grabbed the baby and ran off into the darkness!”

“Torches, we need torches!” Charlie pleads.

“Under the stage!” Ma Rainey points down.

Dmitry squeezes in under the stage and finds a box with torches. He re-emerges and gives one to each guest and they put together a hunting party to catch the Eternal Boxer.

CHAPTER THIRTY-ONE

I'm sprinting through the African darkness with the baby in my arms, trying to reach my secret cave. The cave that is the source of my power. Deep inside the hills where I do my magic.

The bump on the baby's head is screaming bloody murder and the bumps on my head are trying to calm it down.

My bumps come up with a poem on the spot and recite it to the baby.

Oh lunatic moon
Your wise white wink
Your gloom
Curse thee and thy splendorous glitter
Curse thee and thy generous shine
And look upon this world so bitter
And taste these crimson tears of mine.

The stars and moon are so bright that I can make out general shapes on the ground. I carefully jog up a path that's been there for a hundred years.

I climb a cliff face. The child wakes up and starts screaming again and its screams echo down the rocks and throughout the prairie.

The wedding party is after me. I see their torches coming in my direction fast. A whole mob of them in the prairie. And there's two torches in the sky, whizzing around hectically. It's Dmitry and Charlie, flying to catch me.

I make it to the top of the hill and to the entrance to my cave. The angry wedding party is close on my heels and I have no time to waste.

I run into my cave, all the way in until I reach my room. There is a cot here and a fire, which I sometimes use to box against my own shadow.

I draw a circle in the sand and place the baby within it. Then I draw ancient runes all throughout the circle.

I have many vials with many different magical ingredients in them such as Dittany, Mandrake and Unicorn blood. I use a secret combination to open a portal in time. The wedding party has found the cave and is entering it.

"They went in here!" I hear Dmitry yell.

"This way!" Charlie screeches.

I step into the circle with the baby and begin reciting.

"Relicta mater pueri. Aperi portal in hoc tempore. Ego sum fortis. Non est mediocris fabula. Non est deus alius. Non est scientia."

"The mother abandoned the child. Open this portal in time. I am outside myself. There is no fairy tale. There is no other God. There is no science."

A purple portal opens up within the magical circle and grows in size.

Charlie and Dmitry fly into my chamber with absolute horror on their faces just as I and the baby disappear into the portal with a loud BANG.

They fly face first into the wall that I use for shadow boxing and they hurt their noses.

CHAPTER THIRTY-TWO

It is summer 1974 and the G.O.A.T is training for his biggest boxing match at his ranch in Alaska. He is tall and slim and his skin is brown and he has a goatee. He's sparring now and talking shit to his sparring partner.

"You know why you can't beat me? Because I'm the damn G.O.A.T! I'll eat whatever you give me. I'll climb the steepest mountain and never lose my footing. I never sleep, I just shut my eyes and lean against a tree. I am the G.O.A.T, man, I am me!"

His sparring partner is bald and has a spiral serpent's tail. He is taking a real beating and is bleeding from his nose. But he's a humanoid serpent robot so it doesn't really matter.

There is no trainer. "I train myself!" Exclaims the G.O.A.T and the onlookers all applaud.

The onlookers are groupies mostly. Cute girls dressed in flower dresses and fat male journalists with pencil and paper. They all look the same. There's lots of them. They don't matter.

The sparring goes on for another hour until the bald serpent robot is completely ripped apart and just stands on one leg and sniffs and has no arms left.

The G.O.A.T is tired and sends everyone home. Then he pours himself a glass of orange juice and drinks it. "Ah fuck it." He downs the whole bottle.

He takes a shower.

He's about to go to bed when the doorbell rings.

He curses. "Fuck. Shit. Fuck."

The training camp is large and the front door is far away. It takes him a few minutes to get to it. He opens it and catches a glimpse of a funny looking drag queen in a red dress with lots of large potato like bumps on her head hopping away into the forest.

He frowns and then looks down. There's a basket with something in it that's wrapped in a blanket and from the blanket he hears a quiet squealing. He kneels and unveils a little baby girl. She's so adorable and giggles. But she has a bump on her head and the bump has eyes and a nose and a mouth and is staring at him angrily.

"You're a tough one aren't you?" He says.

There's a note in the basket. He opens it and reads it out loud.

"Dear G.O.A.T. I'm sorry that I beat you to a pulp. Here is a gift for you. This time I'm a girl. Teach her to love people."

THE END

Andy Siege

Andy Siege born as Andreas Madjid Siege in Kenya in 1985 is an award winning film director and writer. His debut feature film "Beti and Amare" which he wrote and directed was nominated for multiple high profile international film awards. He has a BA in Creative Writing and an MA in Political Science. He wrote his first novella when he was 14 but it got him in a lot of trouble and then he lost it. LOVE PEOPLE is his second novella.